# Black Rabbit

I0740179

Also by Angus Gaunt and published by Ginninderra Press
*Prime Cuts* (Mockingbird)

Angus Gaunt

# Black Rabbit

For Meredith
with thanks and love

*Black Rabbit*
ISBN 978 1 76041 901 1
Copyright © text Angus Gaunt 2020
Cover image: Emily Hunt

First published 2020 by
**GINNINDERRA PRESS**
PO Box 3461 Port Adelaide 5015
www.ginninderrapress.com.au

'I never heard of a crime I could not imagine myself committing'
Johann Wolfgang von Goethe

# 1

When they open the door to the funeral car, there is someone already inside. The car is a grand old Wolseley, black, of course, with long, gleaming lines, its interior laid out like a London taxi. There is a wide plush bench of green leather faced, behind the driver, by a special seat, a jump seat, that can be pulled down as required. The stranger, for none of them has seen him before, occupies this jump seat. He does not speak as they climb on board. He does not even seem to look up. Sobered more by his presence than the spirit of the occasion, Maurice and his sisters take their own places in silence. They are in car number two, just behind the hearse itself, which is occupied, as protocol seems to dictate, by the driver alone. The stranger's presence means there is no room for Maurice's son. In a rare show of independence, he relegates himself to the car behind, waving away the various suggestions of his aunts. The effect of this rearrangement ripples its way down the cortège until finally dispersing into the first spare place among the cars of lesser rank. It does not take long. Although the cortège itself consists of three Wolseleys, the rest of the procession would be hard pressed to muster the same number of vehicles.

The stranger sits angled over crossed forearms and knees, as though it's his aim to take up the least possible space. The collar of his shirt rises up over his jacket, cradling a round head with two mandibular cheeks. He could be hunchbacked, or without a neck, it is difficult to tell. His shoes are newly polished, with cracks in the toe leather, and his head bears the stunned, slightly discomfited appearance of a recent haircut. Evidently he has gone to some trouble to make himself neat for the occasion. This is one of the reasons Maurice does not question his assumption of a place in the main car. But there is also something else, something strangely intimidating about his presence and the fact that he clearly feels no obligation to explain.

The obvious explanation is that he has some connection with the aunt they are laying to rest and the vast areas of her life of which Maurice and his sisters know nothing. But this was never of much interest when she was alive and it has changed little with her death. Maurice amuses himself, for the time being, with more entertaining speculation. Perhaps he has accidentally joined the wrong funeral party and has not yet realised his mistake? Perhaps he is some sort of crank with a penchant for intruding on other people's grief? Perhaps he simply wants a free ride across town and has surmised that his presence is unlikely to be questioned? Whatever the reason, he has achieved what Maurice will later joke to be the almost impossible feat of silencing his sisters. Their talk is turned off like a tap the moment they climb on board and only resumes, with a circumspect remark or two, once the journey is well under way. It is a not unwelcome state of affairs to Maurice, as it provides the occasion with a decorum that might otherwise be lacking.

The stranger, having failed to acknowledge them as they entered the car, continues in the same vein for the rest of the journey. Once or twice, he lifts his head and looks out of the window, in the manner of someone who is late for an appointment but aware that there is nothing they can do about it, but for the most part he sits with his head bowed, examining his well chewed nails. Now and then, a nervous tic in his throat makes it look as though he is trying to stretch the underside of his jaw. This happens with a sudden, compacted violence that never fails to alarm the observer. It appears to cause him discomfort too, judging by the brief pained look that passes across his grey eyes each time.

When he first took his seat, Maurice had considered coercing a response by the simple expedient of introducing himself. Normally this would be his first step in a situation like this, as an instinctive way of gaining the upper hand, but the unexpectedness of the stranger's presence has somehow short-circuited Maurice's normal conduct. An introduction now becomes increasingly hard to carry off. Having failed to do so at the start, Maurice finds himself unable to do so at all without handing him whatever advantage there is to be gained.

Further into the journey, his sisters start talking again, an oblique resumption of their interrupted conversation. As if in response, the stranger slides a hand into his coat pocket and takes out a small pack of rolling tobacco. The same hand darts back in and emerges this time with a single cigarette paper attached to the thumb. For a moment, Maurice wonders how he has managed to retrieve a single paper like this, then he recalls how, with his tongue, the stranger had already moistened the end of that thumb. It had been the briefest of gestures, almost like a variant of the tic they'd already seen, but it had been sure and deliberate. With the paper adhering to his thumb like a piece of shredded skin, he flips open the top of the bag and starts the process of kneading the tobacco, using just the fingers of a single hand. A sweetish, leathery aroma is released. Having measured out the correct amount, he now brings the paper into play with the deftness of a conjuror. He spreads out the flakes along the paper's crease, scissors it together with two fingers, then lifts it to his mouth to be kissed into life. Or so it seems. Maurice has found himself captivated by the whole process. In the way he dabs his tongue along the paper's edge, he sees, for the first time, the stranger as a human being.

At this time the smoke-free zone is proliferating across the country like a benign, cleansing spore. There is a small, polite notice to the effect on the back of the driver's seat, as befits the discreet atmosphere of the hearse, but even if he has not seen it, as he might reasonably claim, there can be no excuse for him lighting up mid-journey, as it has been generally accepted for some years now that smoking is not permitted on public transport of any kind. Even if this was not the case, the most elementary manners would oblige the smoker to request permission from his fellow passengers before lighting up. So his subsequent action, of producing a throwaway lighter from the same pocket and igniting the thin tube that now trembles between his lips, is more or less the equivalent of spitting on their shoes. And so Maurice is presented with a second opportunity of making contact.

He clears his throat quietly. 'Excuse me,' he says, 'I wonder if you'd mind not smoking.'

The words come out more or less as he intends, firm but polite, with a slightly inflated poise to establish the distance and the element of surprise by which a stranger can normally be made to accept his authority. Whether or not this one is amenable to the tactic is not possible to say, for he acts as though he has not heard Maurice at all, which could hardly be the case, unless he is deaf, which is, Maurice supposes, a possibility. He continues to stare out of the window while a thread of grey smoke forms a connection between the end of the thin paper tube in his fingers and the slowly billowing cloud above his head.

The smell quickly overwhelms the enclosed space. Maurice clears his throat again. He is not usually diffident at times like this but something about this fellow, his brittle shell of self-containment, suggests he should be disturbed with caution. He is leaning forward to reaffirm his point when the younger of his sisters leans out further still and taps the man on the knee.

'Would you put that out,' she says. 'You're not allowed to smoke in here.'

In her voice is a measure of justified indignation which a man would not be able to deliver in a situation like this without suggesting a threat. Nevertheless, Maurice feels vaguely emasculated. He doesn't normally have trouble dealing with this sort of thing. The stranger jumps as though suddenly awakened. He looks up for the first time. His head, resting in the collar of his plain brown shirt, brings to mind a bird on a nest. Maurice's sister shows that her thoughts have been running along similar lines to his by elaborately miming the stubbing of a cigarette. As she pushes her fingers down into the palm of her hand, the stranger stares as though expecting to find a hidden, deeper meaning in her actions.

'No smoking in here!' she repeats, stripping the message down to its essentials.

It is another possibility, Maurice supposes, that he does not speak English – a slight one, but it would give rise to the prospect of a whole series of misunderstandings that might have led to him being here.

Without making eye contact with any of them and without any particular sign that he is about to comply with her demand, the stranger now holds the cigarette side-on to the palm of his left hand and pinches with the thumb and fingers of his right just below its lighted tip. This action would be safer and more efficient if he had fingernails to pinch with, but as it is he must be in danger of burning the raw bulbous flesh where they have been bitten away. This does not seem to bother him. A single deft movement and the little glowing ball finds its way out of the top of the tube and onto the floor, where it smoulders briefly before being smothered by his shoe. He now places the unsmoked portion back in his coat pocket and resumes staring out of the window. The nervous tic returns.

Maurice is still drawn to make contact with him. Once or twice, he finds himself leaning forwards in his mind, holding out his hand and saying his name, but the nearest he comes to translating these thoughts into action is an almost imperceptible shifting in his seat. Diffidence is not normally Maurice's way, but the stranger looks so miserably unavailable to outside stimulus that he feels he would be crushing something, cracking this painstakingly constructed shell, if he so much as opens his mouth. And because by now the murmur of his sisters' conversation is starting to relieve the silence, he decides to ignore him for the rest of the journey.

*

Technically, Maurice and his sisters are the chief mourners, although this hardly seems the appropriate term for people so little affected by the death in question. Their aunt – their great-aunt – has never been much of a presence in their lives. As children, their main exposure to her had been as an occasional and somewhat tiresome visitor, collected from her room in one of the neighbouring towns for Sunday lunches when they could be assured of the buffering presence of a grandparent or two. Meal over, and as soon as decently possible, she would be returned to her lair for a few more weeks or months, to guarded sighs of relief from both their parents. Even then, she came with a vague association of guilt. This was alluded to after every visit when their mother would express her habitual remorse for poor Aunt Patricia's lot in life and her determination that they should have her over a bit more often. She was always 'poor' Aunt Patricia, hardly ever plain Aunt and certainly never anything so jauntily familiar as Auntie. Although no one ever put their finger on it, this sobriquet provided the main evidence of what seemed to be the principal fact about this aunt of theirs, that there was something irremediably wrong with her.

Later, parentless, grandparentless and heads now of their own households, Maurice and his sisters shared the same duties with this fragile relic of their family, who seemed somehow preserved in time and who showed no sign of following the ancestral tendency towards slightly premature death. Generally speaking, the lunches became family occasions at the house of his elder sister, while Maurice's contribution was to fetch their aunt in his car and drive her home afterwards. They imagined these as golden years for Aunt Patricia as they discharged their obligations with a scrupulousness that had been lacking in their parents' time. (Once, his sister had even tried her as a babysitter, but it had not been a success.) They reminded themselves that if it was not for them she might see no one at all, and this was a fate no one could wish on even the most unappealing relative. The arrogance of this assumption was built on a delicately contrived ignorance, for none of them cared to inquire too closely into her life during the weeks that passed between the visits.

Her death, from natural causes at the age of eighty-three, evoked little more in Maurice and his sisters than the slightly guilty recognition of a burden removed. They no longer had to think about her, how long it had been since her last visit and whether she would notice if they put it off for another week or two. Whether she ever did they never could tell, for she had always expressed the same combination of surprise and delight when they phoned to make the arrangement.

The arrangements for the funeral were made with a similar combination of guilt and relief. They could have gone down the budget path, the path that was tailor-made for maiden aunts who have outlived their families – plain pine coffin, an hour's use of one of the lesser hearses, a few empty words in a nondescript crematorium chapel before a hasty consignment to the efficiency of the gas jets. But it was not Maurice's way to be seen looking at the bottom of any price list, even for poor Aunt Patricia with her docile acceptance that she could never be a person worth spending money on. His elder sister had similar thoughts, thoughts to which she was imprudent enough to give voice, thus allowing Maurice to offload the blame, if not the cost, of the extravagance that ensued. Between them they paid for a three-hearse cortège, a coffin of polished walnut and enough flowers, in their cousin's phrase, to deceive a casual observer into thinking a minor movie star was being laid to rest. One of them discovered that their aunt had been an irregular attendee at a church in the suburb where she had lived for the past few years. The minister hardly seemed to know her but he agreed to perform the service, giving the proceedings a suitably portentous edge.

What would she have made of all this, they ask themselves? No doubt, thinks Maurice, she would have accepted it with the same lack of expectation with which she seemed to accept everything else, assuming it was part of some grander design it was no business of hers to interfere with. Walnut or pine, to her it was all the same. She would have been flattered and surprised, he imagines, at the things that were said about her in the church. She would not have appreciated the generic nature of the minister's eulogy or the hollow ring of his own words and would have been oblivious to the brisk and functional nature of the service itself. He suspects, too, that she would have seen all the flowers and would have accurately, if accidentally, surmised that they were there to satisfy a sensibility far more abstruse than her own.

It is a large old church and even for an occasion as obscure as this there is a sprinkling of attendees aside from the family. They are all of Aunt Patricia's vintage and they seem to blend into the pews and the stonework with the inborn skill of old forest birds. These are people with time on their hands, he assumes, the kind that come to every service, regardless of its purpose. Aunt Patricia's family is represented by Maurice and his son, his sisters, and a couple of seldom seen cousins. His sister has left her own children at home with their father, reasoning, no doubt, that poor Aunt Patricia's passing does not warrant full family attendance.

It is a similar reasoning, he supposes, that accounts for his own wife's absence. She has been leading a committee campaigning for a new school library and the funeral clashes with a meeting with one of the governors at which they are to present their case. It is not, and he tells her this, the sort of engagement that normally takes precedence over a funeral. She counters that it is the most important meeting in the life of this committee, the culmination of the work of many months. But surely, he says, there are others who would be able to present the case? No, no, she insists, it has to be her, this is not something she can leave in the hands of others. Then why not rearrange the meeting for another time? Why not rearrange the funeral? she counters, and before he can argue the impropriety of changing a funeral for the convenience of one of its attendees, she is bolstering her case from a different angle. Patricia was his aunt, she tells him, and she has no memories of her other than their duteous Sunday lunches, which hardly gives her cause to mourn her passing. It would be hypocritical, she declares, to put on black and listen to someone else's half-hearted eulogy for a woman she has never regarded as anything other than a minor inconvenience.

So Maurice's family, small to begin with, is reduced by a third. His son is only too pleased to have a day off school and Maurice himself, it so happens, has plenty of time on his hands at the moment.

The stranger is first out of the car at the crematorium. Considering his demeanour throughout the journey, his exit seems startlingly abrupt. The driver has barely applied the handbrake before he shoots out a hand, depresses the silver door handle and bundles himself out of the vehicle as though escaping from a fire. Maurice and his sisters stay in their seats for a moment, stunned by this sudden activity. The stranger makes his way across the gravel to some trees, where he can be seen lurking for the next few minutes with his cigarettes and his lighter.

'What was that?' exclaims Maurice's younger sister, giving voice to the thoughts of them all.

His other sister shakes her head in shared bemusement. Meanwhile the driver, protocol thwarted, has hurried around from his position to hold the already open door with his lightly gloved hand. Maurice wants to ask him about the stranger; how long he had been there before they arrived, if he had spoken at all, whether he had identified himself even. But the man's stony face shows such a determination to reclaim protocol that Maurice decides not to spoil it by making him talk. They stand around on the gravel, in a sudden dazzle of sunlight, while the rest of the cars pull up. The drivers confer quietly as they await their turn in the chapel.

'What was that all about?' his sister says again, determined to keep her outrage fuelled.

All three of them glance over to the trees. The stranger is pacing now, one hand jabbing the cigarette into the space between his pursed lips, the other thrust deep into his coat pocket. The coat rests across his shoulders like a beetle's wings, beneath which his thin legs take long, ponderous strides. It is as though the time spent in the car has deprived him of some vital nourishment which only this striding can put right. They are joined by Maurice's son and a lone second cousin. This gives his sister the opportunity to describe the journey from beginning to end, which she does with relish, keeping them all entertained until it is time to go in.

'Skin-crawling,' is his other sister's main contribution to the story, and Maurice can see what she means. The stranger must be around their age but his helmet of lead-grey hair somehow gives him the appearance of a prematurely aged boy. The full cheeks, with their scar pits and myriad little blemishes, not to mention the seeming size of his head in relation to his body, only add to the disconcerting impression of a youthful face under the trappings of age.

With a quiet signal, the undertakers now open the hearse doors and slide the coffin out onto a wheeled, collapsible trolley. Two of them take the lead in steering it while a third invites the group to join them as bearers. They guide it deftly into the chapel, hardly seeming to lay a finger on it with their white gloves. Maurice is so entranced by the discreet efficiency of these proceedings that he neglects to keep tabs on the stranger. When he does think to look up, he has disappeared from where he was, pacing amongst the trees. Maurice half expects him to materialise right here, placing his quick-bitten fingers alongside their own on the coffin. But he does not and the four of them add their token support to their great aunt's final journey.

In the chapel, a hymn is playing over a portable sound system. It is 'All things bright and beautiful', a non-traditional version that sounds as fresh as a bunch of flowers. It was chosen by his elder sister, along with a couple of others they thought their aunt might have known, from a small selection of discs at the funeral director's office. She'd had no idea of her musical tastes, or even whether she'd had any. She chose this hymn because she thought it was the song with which Patricia was most likely to be familiar. Maurice, who rarely listens to music, is quite unprepared for what he hears. The harmonies billow forth, swirling about the sparsely filled room like ribbons on a breeze, the unfamiliar arrangements drawing attention to the meaning in words that would normally pass by unperceived. If there were a time for funeral tears, it would be now.

But there are none. As soon as the minister stands to say what has to be said, it is evident that this secondary ceremony can only be an anticlimax, with its emphasis on efficiency and ensuring nothing is done to jeopardise the timing of the next appointment. Aunt Patricia's coffin stands on its plinth at the front of the chapel, its floral extravagance looking increasingly overdone in view of the size of the congregation – most of those who attended the church service have not, understandably, made it this far. Maurice can only feel relief when the curtains close over the polished box and the awful unseen machinery is set in motion. There is a last, forgettable hymn, then it is time to go. Mourners from the next cremation are already gathering at the doors. As they rise to leave, Maurice finds he is having trouble remembering his aunt's face.

**2**

After the cremation they go back to Maurice's sister's house, which is about halfway between the crematorium and his own. A modest spread awaits them, consisting of special offer wine and beer and bite-size sandwiches. Their numbers are down yet again. The anonymity of the church and the crematorium are no longer available and most of those that remain are family. Maurice's son disappears to the room below the main house, sucked into the TV's relieving vortex. Apart from his immediate family, there is a handful of cousins he only ever sees on occasions like this and whose names he normally relies on his wife to remember. There are three or four people he does not know at all, but because they are grouped in a corner of the veranda, he assumes they must be acquaintances of Patricia's, probably from the church. He decides to go and talk to them as soon as he has made his way through the cousins. Although it is not his house, he is one of the hosts, and he likes to be able to put his guests at ease. Because they all know but rarely see one another, there is plenty to talk about – news of other deaths and births, and reminiscences from childhood days. In an outburst of temporary enthusiasm, they even begin talking of more regular reunions. Maurice jokes that there are no more aunts left to die.

When he finally makes his way over to the group on the veranda, he notices a lone figure in the far corner scooping fistfuls of peanuts out of a bowl. It is raining by now and he is looking out across the lawn, where the flowers make little occasional lurches as they are hit by heavy drops from the trees above. Once again, the stranger has taken Maurice by surprise. He had not expected him to make it this far. He seems taller now, although his back still arches mantis-like – the low ceiling of his sister's old veranda makes most people stoop whether or not they need to. He is standing by himself but he looks content enough, with the view and the peanuts. His other hand is plunged firmly into the coat pocket from which he had earlier produced his smoking materials. Maurice hopes he will not try and light up again, but after his behaviour in the car he cannot be sure what he will do. He goes outside and introduces himself.

'Maurice,' he says, giving only his first name in an attempt to impose an affable veneer across any residual awkwardness.

It is a second or two before the stranger produces a hand for him to grasp. When he does so, the fingers are limp and yielding, as though he is not used to this form of greeting. In fact, he appears startled by Maurice's attention, as though he has genuinely expected to be left alone. He mumbles his own name in response but does not try to return Maurice's smile. The nervous tic, a gulping motion, surges across his throat and disappears into his collar.

'Sandy,' Maurice repeats, using the technique by which he has learned to remember people's names.

The stranger clears his throat, in a more controlled form of the movement created by his tic. The effort this costs him suggests to Maurice that his failure to be affable in return is born not of wilful refusal but of simple unpreparedness.

'Sandford,' the stranger corrects him, speaking so quietly that Maurice has to lean forwards to hear.

Maurice repeats the name again, with a brief apology for his mistake. Why, he asks himself, is he apologising? It was not his fault he didn't hear the name correctly. Maurice is not a man who generally feels the need to apologise. He clears his throat again. Sandford sounds like a surname, but because he has followed Maurice's lead and introduced himself with just the one name, Maurice has nothing else to call him. Perhaps, Maurice thinks, the fellow assumes he is the sort of person who goes by his last name and he is simply following suit. After all, 'Morris' the surname is commoner these days than 'Maurice' the first name. He wonders why he had been so anxious to seem affable. It would have been better if he had simply given out both in the first place.

Maurice makes some small talk, bland remarks about the weather and the oddly low veranda ceiling. Sandford watches him, an expression of mild discomfort in his eyes. But he holds his stare without difficulty so that in the end it is Maurice who looks away, sweeping out a hand across the damp garden to draw attention to his sister's horticultural talents. The way his eyes focus he seems to be looking around Maurice at the same time as looking at him. The mild discomfort remains, but he seems to grow in stature as he turns to follow Maurice's hand, so that when they next face each other they are more or less eye to eye.

'Yes, Maurice,' he says.

Something about the way Sandford repeats his name causes Maurice to wonder whether he is making fun of him. He glances into his eyes once more but finds no sign of the expected smirk. All he can say now is that this is a person who validates his own presence. He has no need of Maurice's approval. He seems perfectly self-contained, and content to be left alone, although why he would want to be here in the first place is still a mystery. As he is evidently not one for small talk, Maurice decides he might as well ask him the obvious question straight away.

'How did you know Patricia?'

Sandford gives a shrug and a reply that is lost as soon as it leaves his mouth. A sudden laugh from the other group on the veranda muffles his words, which have been spoken in what amounts to a whisper. Maurice feels slightly affronted that this group, who have no obvious connection with the family, should have established quite such a presence.

He asks Sandford to repeat himself, leaning in towards him as he shows no sign of inclining himself in Maurice's direction. The physical gestures involved in this sort of interaction are usually so subtle they are not even noticed, but it is like a slap in the face when they are actually withheld. To hear what he is saying, Maurice has to crane his neck away from his shoulders.

'Friends,' is all he can make out. Clearly this is not good enough, although it at least establishes, if there was still any doubt, that he has not come to the wrong place.

'Well, I didn't imagine you were her long-lost son!'

Sandford shrugs, and Maurice thinks he detects the beginning of a rueful smile on his lips. This encourages him. It is the first time he has let slip a response that could be described as normal. But before he can probe further, Sandford takes his turn to speak.

'What's this for?' he says, with an abruptness that makes Maurice start.

It is a question anyone else would deliver with some opening of the chest, perhaps a sweep of the hand, some acknowledgement of common ground. But Sandford is not given to expansive gestures. He stays as he was, with his hands in his coat pockets. For him it is a simple question, and he wants to know the answer. For Maurice, it is also a fair one.

'What do you mean?' Maurice thinks he knows what Sandford means but he doesn't see why he should be allowed to get away with a question like this without being made to explain himself.

'This…' He moves his hand, still inside its pocket.

'It's for our aunt.'

'She's not here.'

'This is what you do, when someone dies.' Maurice allows some of his irritation to show.

'What?' Sandford looks puzzled now.

'What do you mean?' Maurice asks him. He is beginning to feel at a disadvantage. Sandford is not playing by any rules he understands

'I mean, what are we supposed to do?'

'Here? Now?'

'Yes.'

'Eat. Drink. Talk. Whatever you want to do!' Maurice throws up his hands. He would like to think Sandford is joking, but he seems quite serious.

'Talk?'

'Yes, it's a gathering of people. It's perfectly all right to talk. It's quite normal.'

'What do we talk about?'

It dawns on Maurice that Sandford was asking a completely different question in the first place. He is actually asking for guidance. He wants to know how to proceed.

'Anything you like,' he says. 'Talk about her. That seems like a good topic of conversation. Do you want me to introduce you to someone?'

'Why?'

'So you can talk to them.'

'But I'm talking to you.'

Maurice would have dismissed him by now were it not for the fact that he is so obviously sincere. He would have withered him with a curt put-down before moving on to the next group. But he feels unable to do so. Even if he did, just for his own satisfaction, it seems unlikely Sandford would understand. They stand together for a few seconds, in a silence that Sandford does not seem to find awkward, until Maurice decides to cut his losses.

'Well, I can't let myself be monopolised by you. I must be getting on,' he says, painfully aware of the jauntiness into which he has slipped, and the obvious untruth of this statement.

He moves smartly on to the church group in the corner. Sandford watches him go.

He plays the church group with ease, moving amongst them like royalty, dispensing quips and light physical contact, drawing in their goodwill like oxygen. They are grey, rumpled and benign. They understand why they are here and they know how to proceed. They are, as he thought, connected with the church, but they seem unable to offer any information about Patricia. Unlike Sandford, they do not seem capable of causing a surprise. After a minute or two, he is bored.

*

The gathering, such as it is, does not last much longer. Once the church group has said their goodbyes, it is not much more than family. They file in and out of the kitchen, retrieving plates and glasses from around the house, while his sisters noisily monopolise the sink.

It is not until Maurice goes downstairs to prise his son away from the TV that he remembers about Sandford. He is still there on the veranda, slowly rolling one of his cigarettes. He looks up as Maurice approaches. It occurs to Maurice that he is probably stranded here, all his potential lifts having now departed. He wonders how he is planning to get home.

'Time to go,' he says breezily.

'Yes,' Sandford says, 'I will go.'

'Actually I was referring to myself,' says Maurice. He had intentionally left the remark open in case Sandford took offence at the suggestion he leave. 'But there is hardly anyone left,' he adds, 'just the family.'

Sandford makes a single nod, then lowers his eyes back to his half-rolled cigarette. Maurice has not intended to say anything more, but there is something dismissive in Sandford's gesture that impels him to seek some form of resolution.

'Where have you got to get back to?' he says.

Sandford says the name of a suburb that is almost en route between this house and his own, a suburb Maurice knows well. Before he can give it a thought, they are talking street names and landmarks, simple facts, the sort of talk that makes no demands, and which they both find themselves grasping with a degree of relief. Neither of them seems inclined to branch out, and after a short time there is the inevitable break, which Maurice fills.

'How are you planning to get home?' he says.

'I don't know.'

Maurice's sense of condescension, not quite fulfilled by the grey church group, now finds its expression. 'Perhaps I could offer you a lift. We seem to be going in the same direction.'

'All right, Maurice.' Sandford nods, as though he is doing him a favour.

The party draws to its close. Maurice is delayed by his sisters, both of whom have several family issues to raise while they peck him on the cheek. Sandford waits in the background. Maurice's son disappears back to the TV room. When at last he is free to make his exit, Maurice has to flush him out again, then he finds himself apologising to Sandford for the wait. Sandford accepts his apology with another nod.

*

In the car, Maurice's son does much of his work for him, pumping Sandford with questions in revenge at being denied the front seat. Sandford stretches out his legs and settles into the soft cream leather in a way that suggests this is the sort of environment to which he aspires. He even takes a cursory interest in the car, asking Maurice about the make and the model. Maurice gives his answers and he nods his approval. This pleases Maurice at first, then it irritates him. After all, who is this fellow to approve or disapprove his choice of vehicle? He has probably never owned one in his life. Out of a sort of defiance, Maurice mentions that he upgrades to the latest model every second year.

'Every second year,' Sandford repeats, emphasising the word second.

Maurice now feels impelled to explain that this is how often the new model comes out, as though he would upgrade annually if he could. Sandford nods and smiles, and now Maurice is annoyed at himself for seeking to impress him. It's not normally like this. Maurice is more used to other people trying to impress him.

He seems more responsive to the boy's questioning. Yes, he lives by himself. No, he is not married. No, he does not own a car, he came by taxi and he would have been quite happy to leave the same way if he had not been offered a lift. No, he does not support any football team. No, he does not play computer games. He does not ask any questions in return and eventually Maurice's son withdraws to the comfort of his earphones. The rest of the journey takes place in silence. Sandford speaks only to give final directions to his building.

It is a small block in a gloomy pre-war style, with bricks the colour of dried blood and small windows whose primary function might have been to prevent too much light getting in. Maurice lived in a similar block himself as a young man, and he remembers collecting Aunt Patricia from a place like this, too, in the years before she went to live with her sister in the house in which she has just died.

To Maurice's surprise, Sandford invites them in. He is about to refuse, which seems the natural course of action, but in the back his son suddenly perks up, removes his earphones and starts to open the door. He must be disoriented and under the impression that they have arrived home, but once he is out of the car, Maurice is faced with the need to call him back in if he is to pass up Sandford's invitation, which would entail a far more explicit refusal than he would otherwise have given. He fails to do so, thus losing his chance of discarding Sandford from his life. In reality, though, he is not averse to inspecting Sandford's living arrangements, has no pressing need to be anywhere for the rest of the afternoon, and might well have accepted the invitation anyway.

Sandford occupies a small room on the ground floor of the building. There are four other doors off a wide dark hallway. There is a grey, fibrous carpet throughout and the white-painted walls have faded to full cream. On the wall are, progressively, the cupboard housing the electricity meters, a small fire extinguisher, and a calendar for the previous year. In his room, there is nothing on the walls, no pictures, no photographs. There are shelves built into a shallow recess next to an alcove that holds a sink and a draining board, but they are almost bare too. There are no books, no sign of a television or radio or any type of sound equipment. There is almost nothing that gives anything away about the owner, unless this is done by its very bareness, and the only thing Maurice can see that might be considered entertainment material is a neat pile of magazines on the carpet next to the wardrobe. The top one is laid face down, hiding its title, but the advertisement on the back, for granite kitchen bench tops, suggests the sort of publication prevalent in dentists' waiting rooms. There is, however, a plentiful supply of ashtrays – Maurice counts four, two of which must have been cereal bowls in a former life, all of them darkly smudged with the ashes of his cigarettes – and a pungent farmyard smell coming from somewhere, which threatens to overpower the more entrenched odour of stale tobacco. But the carpet is clean – it still bears the circular compression marks of a recent machine shampoo – and through the window, framed by a pair of thin, garish curtains, is a view into a small, sunny, paved courtyard. Against the wall opposite the sink is Sandford's bed, single and neatly made. From a point in the carpet's dead centre, it would be possible to reach any of the walls with a couple of strides. It is like the cell of a not-quite-ascetic monk.

'Very neat,' Maurice remarks, for the sake of something to say.

'I haven't been here long.'

Sandford seems to relax now he is in his own territory. He goes across to the alcove where he starts the kettle boiling. Maurice accepts his offer of tea. His son, who does not drink tea, refuses his but is not offered any alternative. He is still standing next to the door, unsure how to behave. It is barely conceivable to him that a single room could be anyone's home, let alone a room as small as this. It occurs to Maurice that he might have been ignorant, up to now, of the existence of such places.

Sandford does not speak while he makes the tea. Without asking Maurice, he pours in milk and stirs three or four spoons of sugar into both mugs. He seems quite unused to having visitors. Maurice finds himself wondering whether he has ever made tea for another person.

'So,' he now says as though seamlessly resuming an earlier conversation, 'you were friends with Patricia?' It is provocative ground, in a sense, but Maurice wants to show he is equal to Sandford's caprices.

Sandford stops stirring and looks him in the face. 'Yes,' is all he says.

'Good,' says Maurice, aware that he has nothing more to add. 'That's nice.'

'We used to have coffee together,' Sandford says suddenly, in a voice as clear as it has previously been subdued. 'Every morning,' he adds, 'in a café.'

With this one phrase, Aunt Patricia's hidden life seems to burst out before Maurice's eyes. Aunt Patricia went to cafés! For a moment, Maurice feels he might as well have been told she'd sold drugs or run orgies.

Her life had appeared so bland and pure and quiet in his mind that the worst daily habit he could have ascribed to her was a liking for a cup of tea. Now her life is revealed as a repository of potentially boundless sophistication. It is hard to adjust to this concept in the midst of a conversation.

'You must have known her quite well then,' is all he can say.

Sandford nods. 'I must.'

'How long had you known her?'

'One and a half years,' he says, with an exactness that takes Maurice by surprise.

If he had said a few years, or a few months, he would be able to classify their relationship appropriately. But the very precision with which he has pinpointed the time frame suggests that their meeting had been some sort of milestone for him, a date embedded in his psyche, a watershed, possibly, of some sort. Together with his demeanour and his appropriation of a seat in that primary car, it speaks of a relationship characterised by the sort of intensity which is usually the preserve – Maurice feels vaguely embarrassed even to have thought of it – of lovers. It is not, of course, an inference he is seriously prepared to admit, but after what he has heard so far he is unsure of the boundaries he should place on what he can believe about his aunt.

'Did Patricia ever come here?' he says.

Sandford stops stirring the tea for a moment, then he gives a slightly bemused shake of the head.

Although he has not been asked, Maurice feels compelled to explain himself. 'Just wondering where else she used to go,' he says.

'I don't think she used to go anywhere,' says Sandford.

There are many more questions Maurice wants to ask, or rather there are many more answers he'd like to hear. He does not really know how to frame the questions and at this stage it seems advisable to move slowly, to keep his curiosity in check. Sandford has already proved himself so transgressive of social codes that a single incautiously phrased remark might forever close doors that are just starting to open. For the time being, in any case, Maurice's ruminations are cut short by his discovery of the source of the wet straw smell.

Beneath the window is what he at first took to be a makeshift table – a piece of masonite board resting on a box-like wooden structure. Indeed, he has already used it as a resting place for his mug. A closer look now reveals it to be a cage, wooden-framed, faced by chicken wire and filled with the stuff, in amongst which he can now see the smudged, twitching nose of a large rabbit. Rabbits, of course, are common enough as pets. Maurice had one or two himself as a child. But he has never known one to be kept inside a house, let alone in someone's bedroom. However, the discovery is not unduly surprising. Sandford, as he has revealed himself so far, is the sort of person he would have been more surprised to find in uneccentric living arrangements. He says nothing for the moment, accepting its presence in the room, as he feels sure he will have to accept other things as long as they remain on his turf. He confines himself to hoping that he will open the window.

Sandford brings over the mugs of tea and sits on the bed, as Maurice and his son are already, at his invitation, occupying the only chairs. He pulls across an ashtray from a small shelf behind him and starts to roll a cigarette. The skin on his hands has the dry, jaundiced appearance of the smoker, but the fingers themselves do this work quite dexterously.

Here they sit, in their strange little tableau. Sandford, evidently, does not consider conversation necessary to the gathering and Maurice is, for the time being, wary of asking him any more questions. His son sits quietly on his chair, using the technique he seems to have developed for situations like this, of being not quite present. Sandford leans back against the wall, sipping his tea noisily. When he swallows, the movement looks much the same as his earlier nervous tic. The boy has not yet noticed the rabbit, as his view is blocked by Maurice's chair. Maurice intends to point it out very soon, if the silence is not broken some other way. For the moment, though, he is content to hold his tongue. He is wondering whether Sandford intends to speak at all and, if so, what he might want to say. But it is hard not to start talking. His every social nerve cries out to end the silence. Eventually, it is his son who does so.

'What are we doing here, Dad?' he asks quietly.

Of course, there is no possibility of Sandford not hearing. Maurice glances at him.

Sandford smiles, sips his tea and places the mug on the ledge behind him. It is not really a smile, though; it is more a quiet demonstration of some secret advantage. 'Want to see the rabbit?' he says.

The boy nods. Sandford leans forward on his bed and removes the masonite board, slotting it into the space between the cage and the wall. Instead of reaching in and picking out the rabbit with both hands, he plunges in just one hand and pulls it out by the ears. It hangs there, frozen, until it is placed on the floor, where it now seems quite happy to lope around the little patch of carpet, occasionally standing on its hind legs to sniff at a higher level.

Maurice's son, who winced at the way Sandford removed the animal, looks interested for the first time. It is quite large for a rabbit, mostly white but smudged and dappled with patches of grey. Can he hold it? he asks. Sandford reaches down with the same hand but before he can reach the rabbit, the boy darts forward and retrieves it with both his. He takes his seat again with the rabbit on his lap, where it sits quietly, ears cocked and spread like the resting blades of a helicopter, nose twitching with tame monotony. He smooths down the ears with both hands. Maurice is drawn to stroke them too. They are velvety and surprisingly hot.

The boy asks questions, more from rote than actual enthusiasm, to which Sandford provides economical replies – it's called Smudge, it's two years old, it was given to him. For various reasons, they have not had a pet for some time. Dogs or cats seem too much trouble in the city and anything else, a fish, a bird or a rodent seems rather pointless. His wife, anyway, swore never to get another pet after their first dog and it has suited Maurice to keep her to her word.

'Does your landlord mind you keeping a rabbit in your room?' Maurice asks, remembering the long list of prohibitions he'd had to read before signing the lease on his first flat.

'I didn't ask. As long as you don't bother anyone, they don't care what you do.'

Suddenly the boy speaks. 'You shouldn't pick it up by the ears,' he says, quite firmly.

Sandford straightens his back a little. 'They don't feel it,' he says.

The boy says nothing. He looks down and strokes the rabbit's ears as though soothing a hurt.

Maurice says, 'It sounds like you've had a lot of flats, or rooms.'

Sandford nods.

'How long have you had this one?'

'I said.'

'Yes,' Maurice says. 'So you did.'

In this way, all his attempts at conversation peter out. He sips his tea. It is like sipping warm syrup, sickly but compelling.

The rabbit relaxes on the boy's lap. He continues stroking the ears, glad to have something to focus on.

Sandford sits back again, staring at the ceiling as though there's no one else in the room. It would feel awkward, except that their host shows no obvious need to converse. Very soon he is reaching inside his suit jacket, which he is still wearing, and once again taking out his tobacco and papers. He hasn't smoked the last one yet, but he spends the next few minutes rolling another leisurely smoke, spreading the tobacco across the paper in a way that suggests the act of making it is just as important as the actual smoking.

Maurice takes a last sip of his own sickly concoction and rises to his feet. 'I suppose we'd better be off,' he says.

Sandford looks up. 'Why?'

'Things to do,' he says airily. 'Come on,' he says to the boy.

As there is no obvious surface on which to place his half-drunk mug, he offers it to Sandford, thus drawing attention to the fact that it's unfinished. Sandford does not seem to notice him and he ends up placing it in the little alcove. Every word, every little action, it seems, is a skirmish in some wider contest between them. Maurice is unable to make a single move without being aware of this, although it is anybody's guess what Sanford thinks. It is unnerving in a way, but also fascinating, and it arouses his instinctual need to be always in the box seat.

The boy lifts the rabbit carefully. He is about to return it to the cage himself but before he can stand up, Sandford has grabbed it by the ears again. He holds it in the air for a moment, just long enough to see another wince of pain pass across the boy's face, then drops it on the straw from a little higher than seems necessary. He does this with the defiant air of someone reclaiming their ground. Defiance breeds defiance.

The boy now says, 'It shouldn't be on its own. Rabbits get lonely, you know.'

Instead of simply contradicting him, as before, Sandford nods slowly. 'Maybe I'll get a companion for it,' he says.

Maurice feels an irrational stab of jealousy. His son has been able to elicit a small bow of respect that he has not yet managed. He mutters the usual platitude about the pleasure of meeting him. Even as he says the words, he is conscious of their untruth in a way he never normally would be. At first he thinks they are going to leave without any acknowledgement from Sandford, but then, as Maurice is poised holding the half-open door through which his son has just disappeared, he speaks.

'Did you love her?' he says.

'What?' Maurice has the feeling he has been here before. He is standing there with his other hand on the door knob, a globe of well-worn ceramic attending a clumsy mechanism that grinds against discretion.

Sandford raises his head and locks eyes with him. In the fading light his grey irises almost disappear. 'Did you love her?'

'She was family,' Maurice says.

'Did anyone love her?'

'We did what we could for her.'

Sandford does not reply.

'My sister wanted to give her the send-off,' Maurice says. 'I just helped pay for it.'

He closes the door and marches smartly out of the house. The old lock rattles loudly.

32

**3**

Maurice is currently, as he puts it, 'between jobs'. For many years, he has worked in the finance industry. When asked what he does, he will describe it thus: the world is awash with money, spare cash floating around the globe in search of a temporary resting place; the players in the industry work day and night to exploit this knowledge, constantly on the lookout for new ways to extract another fraction of a percentage point from some notional stash that has come to rest somewhere for a few hours, continually trying to outdo one another by devising new strategies, new formulas, new products. It is an industry that lavishly rewards success. He will contend that out of the owners of any ten large homes in the wealthiest parts of this city, it would be a safe bet that seven of them are involved in financial services in one form or another.

Before taking up his last position, a job he took more to satisfy his wife than himself (after he had been without work for two months following a long-sought redundancy), he started to develop a scheme he had been considering for some time. It exploited time lags, taxation and obscure government regulations in a dark recess of the insurance industry. With two partners, an accountant and a corporate lawyer, he now continued working on it in his spare time. For a year, they met every night to work on their strategy. Maurice believed it would make him one of the wealthiest people in this city, a claim he repeated to his wife whenever she complained about his long hours. Then one day his CEO called him in. He was letting him go, he said. He had breached the terms of his employment contract by working in secret on his own project. Maurice was outraged – it was not a job he had particularly wanted in the first place and if there was any terminating to be done, it should have been done by him. Furthermore, there was to be no redundancy payout this time, a position they were prepared to have tested in court.

His first instinct was to sue them for wrongful dismissal, if for no other reason than to force them into a private settlement to make him go away, but it quickly became clear that his case was weak. He then thought he had a basis on which to fight when he discovered they had begun developing his scheme, or something almost identical, themselves. There was no clause in his contract that allowed them to claim the rights to the work he was not supposed to be doing while he was in their employ. But after spending several months and a large proportion of the value of his earlier redundancy payout, he realised he was not going to win, whatever the merits of his position. Every time there seemed to be a chink in their case, a glimmer of hope, they poured money into the gap like concrete. He could not compete, even with his lawyer partner working, as she did for a time, pro bono. He was simply unable to match their resources and if he did not really appreciate it before, he appreciates now that a legal stoush is nothing to do with a battle of right versus wrong; it is a battle of resources.

Sometimes, when looking for a possible explanation for the ease with which Sandford was able to insinuate himself into his life, it is to this that Maurice looks. Like a virus, he slipped in while his immune system was weak. Maurice has never been a doormat to anyone; in his dealings with others he is accustomed to getting his own way, and if he is not able to do so immediately, the fight is on. It is a stance that has served him well in his career, where he has always seen his colleagues as obstacles and rivals rather than allies. Yes, it is true to say that the spirit of compromise has not smouldered strongly in his psyche. And yet here is a person who appears to bear all the hallmarks of someone over whom he would normally ride as easily as a flea, and he has had neither the ability nor the desire to do so. It's alarming, but also strangely fascinating. He feels agreeably helpless, as though being slowly pulled into a vortex.

Maurice is now looking for work, and it is proving harder than he had thought. He has been following the industry from afar, watching the progress of 'his' scheme. When the government regulations it was exploiting unexpectedly change, and its positive returns start to reverse, he becomes aware of a certain damage to his reputation. Even though he never had a chance to put the scheme into practice himself and he no longer has anything to do with it, its failure is somehow inextricably linked with him. He did not understand it at first, but now he realises his antagonists have influence which is wider and subtler than he has given them credit for. A little dirt fed into the grapevine has spread across the industry and tarnished his name. People in his network, for whom a single phone call is usually enough to set in train a series of events that results in him being offered a lucrative new position, now seem to be avoiding him. These are people with whom he has enjoyed extravagant lunches, long afternoons in the sun revelling quietly in their shared detachment from the common run of things. Now they are out when he calls, they don't return his phone messages, they ignore his emails.

This is what most troubles him about what has happened – more than the loss of his scheme, his job, his income, he has discovered that he is not, after all, an untouchable. For years, Maurice has been a man of influence, a man who hires and fires, a man whose word can make or break the careers of others. Absorbed by his power over the people in his reach, he has denied the very existence of those who can make or break him.

Now for once he has found himself pondering the motives of other people. Strangely, indeed self-defeatingly for someone so drawn to get the upper hand, he has never paid much attention to what drives others. It has always been enough, for him, to have his plan and to put it into operation regardless of anyone else. Now he is starting to see that, as in a game of any kind, there are tactical advantages to be gained from understanding one's opponents and rivals.

His attempts to understand his erstwhile colleagues begin to spread once he finds himself at a loose end. He begins to wonder about the motivations of all those he deals with, the people he buys things from, the people he pays to do things for him, the people he meets during the course of his day. He is surprised by the amount of information that can be elicited from a casually dropped remark. He is rather taken aback at the number of people who need only the smallest nudge to pour out their life story. He starts to enrich his daily interactions by starting conversations where normally he would complete his business without a second thought. He becomes firm friends with the couple who run the newsagency, he learns the names of his cleaner's grandchildren, he exchanges a willing ear for local gossip with the woman in the dry cleaner's and talks sport and politics with the man who mows the rugby oval.

In doing this, he learns little to his direct advantage, but he appreciates the way these exchanges are able to oil the wheels, so to speak, of his day. He finds himself surprised, constantly, by the opinions and insights that emanate from the mouths of these people, people who have previously registered with him as little as though they were tools or machines. There is a downside, of course, those times when he is in a hurry or does not feel like chatting. But when required, he becomes adept at cutting short these conversations without giving offence. He learns to dispense a simple bon mot, or offer a condescendingly frank observation before making his flying excuse. It is not hard and it opens up his life to a dimension he would not otherwise have known existed. In any case, he is rarely in a hurry these days.

*

He neither sees nor has any contact with Sandford over the next couple of weeks and it is true to say that, if he had not had time on his hands, Sandford would have disappeared from his radar. As it is, he cannot forget him and the way he so easily assumed the upper hand. Yes, he did not concern himself with social niceties but that has hardly been something outside Maurice's experience. There must have been something else to have brought forth the response he did. A part of Maurice wants to experience this again, just to observe how it comes about, understand its mechanics, as it were. Sandford has come to represent a piece of unfinished business. Thus it is that the phone call he receives later that week is not entirely unwelcome.

'Hello, Maurice?' says the voice at the other end.

'Yes,' he responds warily, as he always does when it is a voice he does not recognise.

This one has a slight accent, possibly Indian, and his first reaction is that it must be a cold marketing call. Maurice instinctively recoils when he is addressed by his first name like this. He resents the caller's assumption of this unearned familiarity, the crude attempt to place him under an obligation to be matey in return and therefore less likely to refuse to listen to what he has to say.

'You don't know me,' the voice continues, 'but I am the owner of the building in which Patrick Sandford is a resident.'

It takes Maurice a moment or two to register the name. Sandford has never mentioned his first name and Maurice has only ever thought of him, as he will continue to do, in terms of his last.

'You are his relative, I believe?'

'We're not related.'

'Friend then.'

'I've met him once,' he says, unwilling to let this go. 'Why are you calling me?'

'Well, Mr Maurice, the fact is that Patrick has left you his rabbit.'

Does Maurice detect a trace of amusement in the way he imparts this information? No, he is playing it straight. It is simply his over-enunciation that suggests irony.

'I'm sorry,' he says. 'I have no idea what you are talking about. Are you saying he's died and left me a rabbit?'

'Not died. Patrick Sandford has disappeared.'

'How could he have left me his rabbit then?'

'He left a note.'

'A suicide note?' Although he knows almost nothing about him, it strikes Maurice that of all the people he has known, there could be no one whose suicide would surprise him less.

'Just a note,' says the landlord, 'a short note.'

'What did it say?'

There is a pause, during which Maurice imagines the man putting on his glasses.

'"Maurice will look after the rabbit",' he reads. 'Then he writes your telephone number.'

'Is that all?'

'That is all.'

'Look,' Maurice says, 'I hardly know the fellow. I've only ever met him once.'

'Mr Maurice,' he says, 'I have no liking for the damn creatures but it would be grossly unfair to leave it alone in that room. I have no idea where our friend has taken himself off to or when he intends to return. His rent is paid until the end of next week. His door was left ajar. He intended the rabbit to be discovered and handed over to you. This is what I am now doing. My only alternative is to take the unfortunate creature to the vet.'

'All right,' Maurice says, 'I'll come over.'

He could, he supposes, have told him to go ahead with his suggested alternative. After all, none of this is his business. But once again, Sandford seems to be drawing him in. Why has he chosen Maurice to look after the rabbit? The only think he can think is that he had intended it for his son, possibly as some sort of payback for daring to protest when he picked it up by the ears. It seems unlikely that Sandford would know many people. With Patricia's death, perhaps Maurice is his only option? Whatever, he cannot see the harm in taking it home with him. The boy would enjoy having a pet of his own and, even though his mother would no doubt raise objections, there is room enough in their yard for her to be barely affected by its presence.

He goes over that evening. The landlord is waiting for him. He wears suit trousers and a white business shirt with two buttons open. It still bears ironing creases, as though he has changed before coming to meet Maurice, as though this is his idea of relaxation, to go tieless after a hard day's work.

His name is Mr Agarwal. He shakes Maurice's hand. 'I do appreciate this, Maurice,' he keeps saying, producing small flecks of spittle from his long, fleshy lips.

Maurice follows him into Sandford's room. It is much as it was before. The mugs from which they drank their tea are on the shelf next to the basin, washed up and gleaming together. The rabbit is there, of course. When they enter the room, it comes lolloping out of its lair, standing up on its hind legs and sniffing the air with its pink, querulous nose. The window is now open, but there is no disguising the fact that an animal has been shut up in here on its own for several days.

'I only just opened the window,' says Mr Agarwal.

'I wonder why he didn't leave it open to begin with?'

'He probably wanted to draw attention to the smell. Coupled with his failure to lock his door, this indicates to me a desire that the animal be discovered as quickly as possible.'

The answer occurred to Maurice as soon as he had finished posing the question and he really does not need the man to supply it. His precise and ponderous English is already beginning to get on Maurice's nerves, but he is determined to suppress his natural reaction – to override these musings with his own – on the off-chance that he will be more rewarded by treating him with a sort of humorous indulgence.

'You sound like a detective, Mr Agarwal,' he says.

The man grins briefly, then coughs and turns his attention elsewhere as though unable to decide whether Maurice is making fun of him or not. 'I have not been able to work out how long it is since he abandoned the place,' he says.

'When did you first notice he'd gone?'

'It was not me, it was one of the other residents. He telephoned me this morning. He told me he had noticed that Mr Sandford's door had been ajar for a day or so before he finally plucked up the courage to see what was going on.'

'That means he's been gone since at least yesterday morning. That would be Thursday. I saw him here on Monday evening, so he must have left some time in between. He's done a little bit of cleaning up since then, so I would guess he left on Tuesday, or possibly Wednesday.'

Mr Agarwal nods eagerly. He seems to like this kind of talk. 'Do you think we ought to call the police?' he says.

'He's not exactly missing, is he? I mean, he might have just gone away for a few days.'

'But the note, and leaving the door ajar.'

'Is that really all the note said?'

He produces the note from his shirt pocket. It is on a large piece of A4 paper, torn from a lined pad. The only words, in neat capitals, are the ones he has quoted.

'It seems very odd,' is all Maurice can say.

'Odd,' says Mr Agarwal. 'That is exactly what I thought.'

He helps Maurice carry out the hutch. Although it appears quite large on the floor of Sandford's room, it is comfortably narrow enough to fit through the various doorways. Even so, they manage to scrape paint off the door jambs in several places mainly due, Maurice notes, to Mr Agarwal's clumsiness. But it does not seem to worry him and, as he is the landlord, it does not worry Maurice either. They decide to leave the rabbit in the hutch rather than transport it separately.

Mr Agarwal is in favour of keeping it on the other side of the wire at all times. 'Nasty blighter,' he says. 'With those teeth, it could give one quite a nip!'

It turns out that he has never actually handled a rabbit before and has never heard of anyone being bitten by one. His distrust seems directed at animals in general.

'It mystifies me why anybody would want to keep such a creature as a pet,' he says, as he stretches his back after the hutch has been safely deposited across the back seat of Maurice's car. 'And yet Mr Sandford was evidently quite attached to it, even to the point of making arrangements for it before he disappeared.'

'A pity he didn't just ask me,' Maurice says. 'After all, he had my number.'

'I expect he didn't want to alert anyone too soon to his intention to disappear.'

They go back to the room, so that Mr Agarwal can write down his number for Maurice, in case Sandford contacts one of them. Then he leaves, pleading another appointment. Neither of them wants to be the one to go to the police, with all the undoubted hassle it would entail, even though Maurice feels it is more the landlord's responsibility than his own. After all, he has only met him once and a week ago he'd been unaware of his existence. They agree to leave it for a few days, after which they can confirm that he really is missing.

'Can he actually be a missing person,' Maurice says, 'if nobody misses him?'

Mr Agarwal thinks this a great joke, and shakes his hand heartily before taking his leave.

*

Mr Agarwal has not expressed any intent to lock up Sandford's room, nor did he ask Maurice to do anything about it before he left. He has simply left him here with the room open, as though it is his prerogative, as keeper of the rabbit, to take a final snoop around. Maurice thinks he may as well do so. Aside from anything else, he might find a clue as to where Sandford has gone. He likes the idea of playing detective.

There is not a lot of snooping to be done. Sandford's room is tiny and it is not abundantly furnished, either by furniture or personal possessions. Without the rabbit hutch, which has left a mild indent on the grey carpet, there is nothing more than the bed, a chair, and a flimsy white wardrobe. If Maurice had known nothing at all about the person who lived here and wanted to reconstruct his life from its contents, he would hardly know where to start. The three drawers on one side of the wardrobe contain, as expected, his clothes, very few in number and almost as unremarkable as it is possible for clothes to be. The only item of note is a blue business shirt, a pricey brand that Maurice sometimes buys for himself, roughly folded among socks and cheap T-shirts displaying bland and forgettable designs. Another thing he notices is that there is no underwear. Maurice experimented with no underwear for a time, and found it pleasantly liberating until his wife noticed and reacted as though he was indulging in some sort of perversion. A more likely explanation, he thinks, is that Sandford has taken his underwear with him, along with all the other clothes he is likely to need wherever he has gone.

In the other side of the wardrobe he finds, neatly arrayed on hangers, a business suit and several more shirts. There is a musty smell. The suit trousers have the same mud stains as appeared on his own after the service. The only other thing in here is the pile of magazines. Maurice leafs through them: photography, yachting, celebrity gossip and fashion – many genres are represented. Most of them are old and creased, suggesting they were not bought new. Here and there is evidence of pictures, or whole pages, having been torn out. Maurice wonders what a skilled investigator might make of these observations. He suspects, too, that the paltry furniture is not Sandford's, that it has been lent by the landlord, or left behind by the previous occupant, or perhaps even cobbled together from council clean-ups, to be returned to the kerbside when he moves on.

Sandford's room may be small, but he has been barely able to fill it. Standing there amongst his things, with so few signs of his presence, Maurice has the impression that he would have preferred it to be smaller, that it has dim reaches on which he has been unable to impose himself. Yet it contains all that is needed to sustain a single life. Maurice's own first flat was much bigger, but he still remembers the feeling when he first closed his door on the outside world, the comfort of being able to burrow into his own little domain. He has the same feeling, sometimes, in hotel rooms. In his own house, with its many bright rooms, he has never felt it.

He closes the wardrobe door and stands up straight. With the window open a pleasant scent of autumn jasmine comes through. It is growing from a wine barrel which, along with a mouldy-looking director's chair, is the only other thing on the roughly tiled terrace outside. The plant has gained a tenuous hold on the brickwork next to the window but most of it is spreading across the ground. Cigarette ends abound beside the chair. They are filterless and home-rolled, undoubtedly Sandford's, but they all seem to be recently discarded, leading Maurice to suppose that either someone cleared them up periodically or Sandford has not been smoking out here long enough to leave much history.

**4**

As her closest living relatives, it falls upon Maurice and his sisters to dispose of their aunt's possessions. It is a task they take to with alacrity. The three of them meet at Patricia's house one weekday morning. It's a three-bedroom terrace in a quiet street in a suburb close to the city, the sort of house that could have been, and indeed was, picked up for a song some twenty years ago and is now, thanks to the rejuvenation of what had once been dismissed as slums, worth a small fortune.

It did not belong to Patricia. It had been bought as an investment by their farming grandparents, the fruit of a few good seasons. After their grandfather died, their grandmother decided to come back to the city where she had lived as a child. She moved into the investment property and invited her sister to live with her. Patricia had been in a boarding house for many years, sharing a bathroom, flimsy walls and a certain degree of communal chaos with an assortment of misfits and eccentrics. It took some persuasion to get her to move, a reluctance which fuelled the family mythology that she was soft in the head. They shared the house until the death of her sister, a couple of years later. Patricia must have grown attached to the place for she did not now move out, as they were expecting. They discovered that their grandmother had added a clause to her will guaranteeing her sister's occupancy as long as she wanted to stay. And so she had done.

Now the house is theirs and they open the front door with a cautious air of proprietorship. None of them has been inside since their grandmother's death and they are not sure what to expect. Patricia always used to be waiting on a bench next to the front door when Maurice arrived to pick her up, which he took as a sign of her eagerness to embark on an outing which was undoubtedly one of the highlights of her life, and she always insisted on going in alone when he dropped her off, to save him the trouble, she said, of finding somewhere to park.

The house is in much better condition than Maurice expected. The hall appears to have been freshly painted and the carpet is so new it still has its showroom smell. There are aspects of the kitchen that would not look out of place under his wife's auspices. They have already decided to put the house up for auction and as they make their way through it every room, every wall and brick seem to exude the frisson of untapped wealth.

Maurice's sisters scurry through the rooms, shrieking like schoolgirls.

'It's a Bosch!'

'Look at those curtains!'

'These sheets, they're four-hundred ply. Why would she need this many sets?'

'Are you sure this is the right house?'

There is the unspoken suggestion that Patricia is somehow undeserving of the sorts of trappings they would take for granted.

Upstairs it is both more and less of a surprise. There are three bedrooms, with the two largest leading out through double doors onto a balcony which overlooks the street. The decorative cast-iron work on the balcony, which is the main aspect the house presents to the outside world, is badly rusted and even snapped off in places. From this, a burglar might conclude that the house is easy to break into but probably not worth doing so. Neither of these bedrooms had been chosen by Patricia. Hers is the smallest, next to the bathroom at the back of the house, with a view into the unused yard. It presents the same air of ascetic disunity as Sandford's room, with just a single bed, a wooden wardrobe and a bedside lamp whose shade is stained with the effluvia of an old and favoured possession. On a chair in the corner opposite the bed is a portable TV set. There is no mirror and none of the paraphernalia for making up and removing the face that Maurice associates with a woman's bedroom. The bed is unmade, an omission his sisters immediately set about rectifying.

With some trepidation, Maurice opens the doors to Aunt Patricia's large wooden wardrobe. It is sparsely filled, but unlike Sandford's the clothes look as though they have been hanging there for years. The colours of her half-dozen or so nondescript dresses seem to have taken on the dingy hues of the wardrobe's interior, and two pairs of plain brown shoes wait on the floor, ready for the next insertion of those pale, ghost-like feet. A sense of delicacy prevents him from pulling out the drawers, but his sisters have no such qualms. They yank them open and drop blouses, underwear and stockings into garbage bags from which they will be thrown away or at best recycled as rags. There is no chance that any of Aunt Patricia's clothing might appeal to someone new.

All this is done in silence, as though they are all wary of giving voice to the poignancy surrounding these paltry traces of a life. Comment is reserved for the dozen or so large pieces of coloured card Maurice discovers stacked against the cupboard's back wall. He pulls them out and lays them on the bed. Each one is covered with pictures that have been cut with scissors out of magazines. There must be hundreds on each card. Most of them contain faces, photographs of people. Maurice recognises a few, a sportsman here, a film star there, all crowded together and laid over one another like the feathers on a peacock's back.

'The famous collages!' says one of his sisters.

'What do you mean?' says Maurice.

'Her collages. I wondered what they were like. They're not that bad. She was always going on about them.'

'Not to me she wasn't.'

'Well, you didn't talk to her much, did you?'

But I did, Maurice wants to insist, I picked her up and drove her home for all those Sunday lunches; it's not my fault if she didn't want to confide in me. But at the same time he feels strangely snubbed.

His sisters spend a few minutes looking through the collages, pointing out faces they recognise, then, agreeing that no one could possibly have any more use for these things, they fold them into bin-sized squares to be dumped with the other stuff. As they all leave the room, a single brown stocking can be seen coiled from the black lip of one of the garbage bags, like the final ectoplasmic remnant of a soul that never took up its share of space to begin with.

The two front bedrooms are as cluttered and messy as Patricia's is neat and bare. Both rooms are, quite simply, filled with stuff, a vast and haphazard array of it. There is computer equipment, clothing and an electric guitar, there are books and DVDs, there are suitcases, clocks and golf clubs. There are even a couple of expensive-looking bicycles – mountain bikes with thick tyres and elaborate gearing mechanisms. Here and there some sort of order has been imposed – shoes and phones lie in neat piles like fruit in an African marketplace – but for the most part stuff has been thrown in without a thought for its retrieval. It is much the same in both rooms except that there are chairs and tables in the first, their shapes recognisable beneath the clutter like ancient ruins being reclaimed by the jungle, while in the smaller room there is no furniture except a foam mattress and a pillow.

'Aunt Patricia was something of a bowerbird,' says Maurice's elder sister.

'Looks more like she was a second-hand dealer,' says his younger.

'A second-hand dealer? She wouldn't have had the nous!'

'How do you know what she was capable of?' says Maurice. Both sisters look at him strangely. He would look strangely at himself too, if it were possible. It's not the sort of thing he would have said had it not been for the conversation with Sandford.

They wade a little way into the rooms, picking up items that catch their eye. His younger sister gets no further than the shoes, which she picks through with the odd exclamation of approval. She even kicks off her own and tries on a pair or two.

Maurice, in an attempt to explain himself, suggests that their aunt may have been suffering from a mental disorder. 'I've seen it before,' he tells them. 'They can't stop bringing home stuff. Before you know it they've got a house full of rubbish. I knew a house once where the woman used to spend all day collecting cardboard boxes. She had so many piled up in her front yard that you could hardly see the house. Every few months, the council would clean them out and she'd just start again. Hoarders.'

His elder sister nods quietly in agreement, a familiar deference by which he is always gratified.

His younger says, 'But this isn't junk.'

'Some of it is,' says Maurice, unwilling to cede the point.

'It's all worth something to someone. I always wondered what she did with herself. I reckon she was a dealer. I reckon she had a secret life!'

The thought, and the way she says it, makes them laugh. They shuffle through the room, discussing their aunt's capacity to engage in any sort of commercial activity. The only conclusion they come to is that she has surprised them. There can be no doubt that someone has been spending money on the house, and the stuff they are wading through appears to be the likely source of it. But it is hard to see poor Aunt Patricia as the driving force behind an operation of this, or indeed any kind. The idea of a secret life appeals. They start to elaborate. She had a secret lover. She was a burgling mastermind, a Fagin. She was the godmother to a whole criminal fraternity. Maurice, already blindsided by her artistic pursuits and her daily coffee ritual, nods and laughs along.

*

After a closer inspection, Maurice begins to recognise much of the furniture in that second room as that which had been left behind after their grandmother's death. Her will had stated that Patricia be allowed to remain in the house for as long as she wanted, with sufficient of her possessions to maintain her lifestyle. The house had been crammed with furniture at that time because it contained everything from the much larger house they had come from. Maurice remembers the resentment aroused by this clause, that everything should fall into the lap of this wraithlike woman who had not earned the right to such things and would be sure not to appreciate them.

Both his wife and his younger sister had been more forthright, stating that if a bedsit in a boarding house had been good enough for her all those years, it was surely good enough for her now. It was a sentiment Maurice did not dispute. It seemed absurd that she should occupy a good three-bedroom home, and it seemed a waste that she should be steered towards this place when she would be just as accepting of something more modest. But he was determined to honour his grandmother's wishes, and to be seen to do so. He spent a whole day going through the house with Aunt Patricia, diligently observing the terms of her sister's will by marking, with red stickers, all the items she thought were essential to her daily life. Part of his sanction, he felt, was to steer her away from the things already coveted by other members of the family. In this, he was completely successful, for there could have been few people more amenable to suggestion than Aunt Patricia. When the interested relatives arrived the following weekend to claim their booty, there was hardly anything which could be described as in any way desirable that was adorned with one of the red stickers. She seemed quite content. Indeed, it was Maurice who ended up dissatisfied with the distribution, and he found himself forcing one or two things on her, such as the better of the two kitchen tables and an armchair on which he knew his sister had her eye, just to dispel any impression that he might have bullied her.

The next day, they all turned up, Maurice, his sisters and some cousins, to divide up their grandparents' possessions. Those who had them brought their families, the house was packed for the morning and a party atmosphere reigned. Patricia hovered in the background, pouring cordial for the children and offering tea to the grown-ups, which she served sweet and milky and which remained, for the most part, undrunk. Once or twice, they found her seated on a chair or couch as it came up for disbursal, and a thin haze of embarrassment arose. Maurice attempted to diffuse it by suggesting, light-heartedly, that she would be better off only occupying furniture that had been stickered, a proposal she embraced as though it had been a matter of common protocol of which her sheltered existence had left her unaware. She retreated, chastened, to the other side of the room. ('Meanie,' said his sister, unhelpfully.)

By midday, they had finished and every item had a new home. Maurice was pleased that his organisation had resulted in a more or less even distribution of all the items of value. Some adjudication had been necessary, but all in all everyone was content with what they had acquired. Most of them were taking away their new possessions there and then – he had hired a removal van for the purpose – so that by the time they had all left midway through the afternoon, the house looked as though it had been stripped by mysteriously selective locusts. With his wife and a cousin, he helped rearrange what remained. Patricia seemed to have no opinion as to how she wanted the furniture set out. She continued to hover as before, like a ghost. Whatever they suggested, she agreed to it, and if anyone counter-suggested, she agreed with that as well. Eventually they stopped asking her opinion and just arranged the rooms as they saw fit.

It was a similar story upstairs, where the removal of the marital bed had left a large void in the master bedroom.

'I suppose you'd like this as your bedroom now,' his wife said. It was by far the best bedroom in the house.

'That would be nice,' said Patricia.

'We can always leave you where you are, if you prefer,' said Maurice's cousin, sensing an opportunity to get away sooner.

'I'm quite used to my old room,' Patricia agreed.

And so it went on, every further minute of dialogue confirming them in their opinion that this was all wasted on her.

*

Over tea in the kitchen, served in chipped mugs which they are now surprised to find are the best their aunt seemed to have, they debate what to do about the things in the house. The original idea, based on the assumption that everything desirable had already been distributed at the time of their grandmother's death, had been to hire a truck and have the contents delivered, holus bolus, to the nearest charity shop. They had not allowed for the possibility of them becoming desirable again.

'I think we should stick to our original plan,' says his elder sister.

'But there's some good stuff here,' says his younger – she is planning to put down a deposit on a flat with her share of the house's proceeds. 'I could do with that dishwasher, for a start.'

'Keep the dishwasher then. We'll give them the rest.'

'It's OK for you,' she grumbles, 'you've got everything you want.'

'I don't have a Bosch.'

'You could if you wanted.'

'Well, what else do you want?' She rolls her eyes. Their younger sister has long been established as the feckless one in the family.

'Why don't we do what we did before?' Maurice says.

'What, red sticker day? I don't want to go through all that again!'

'Why not? It worked very well, and nobody could complain it wasn't fair.'

In the end, they settle on a modified form of the so-called red sticker day. They open up the house the following Sunday and invite the family to come over and take their pick. His sister marks the items she wants with post-it notes ('Yellow sticker day?' his other sister suggests) and they make a preliminary division of certain items to ensure some degree of fairness – the bicycles, for instance, are earmarked for Maurice's son and the child of a cousin who is a similar age.

The day is brisk and businesslike, with none of the festive atmosphere of the previous occasion. The enthusiasm generated then was related to childhood memories of their grandparents' large, comfortable house, and the promise of their own share of the solid and timeless furniture they had dreamed of ever since. Now all that was gone, safely stowed in the houses of those to whom they are now offering the chance to pick through an obviously inferior class of spoils. Not unpredictably, the only ones interested enough to turn up are the teenage children of their cousin, who spend half an hour or so sifting through the junk, then call their father to help them cart away what they have selected. His sister, meanwhile, has agreed to leave her yellow-stickered items in situ for the time being, because things are changing for Maurice.

*

One of the revelations of this time, for him, is the complexity of the life his wife has made for herself. He finds himself surprised and even faintly envious, although not unhappy, to discover she is rarely at home during the day. Her time is filled, it seems, with tennis, yoga classes, school committees and lunches. All these activities, even the lunch dates, are embarked on with a hint of martyrdom that brooks no opposition. Oh, she tells him, she is busy, so busy she hardly has time to scratch herself. It is an impression she is careful to cultivate now he is at home. When they find themselves together in the house during the day, she disposes of him with a few brisk words before moving onto her next activity, much as he imagines she must have dealt with the tradesmen who have worked on their renovations over the years.

One day, they both find themselves in the kitchen in the early afternoon, so they have their lunch together on the deck where a recent project has afforded them a very expensive view of some trees in a distant valley. Her skin, as she bustles about the room making their sandwiches, retains a glassy sheen from the exertion of a tennis game, and small patches of perspiration still darken her white sleeveless top, from which her browned shoulders emerge fit and self-assured. In earlier times, Maurice might have concentrated his efforts on removing this top preparatory to an hour's semi-illicit lovemaking while their son was at school, but recent history has taught him that any movement in that direction is likely to draw a definitive rebuff. Those browned shoulders are for tennis and the greater glory of her new bodily health, they are not for him. On another occasion, when they are similarly situated, he casually (oh, so casually!) brushes against her forearm with his fingers to see whether it is possible to recapture some of the excitement the feel of her flesh had once engendered, and she flaps him away in the momentary panic of an unknown insect's touch. When she realises it is him, she blushes and lays her hand on his forearm, appeasingly but briefly enough to leave no doubt that for her his touch is little more welcome than that of the imagined arthropod.

They have talked about this, in an oblique and unsatisfactory way. Sex (she even pronounces the word as though it creates a displeasing taste in her mouth) just doesn't do anything for her any more; in fact, she wonders now whether it ever did. All Maurice's arguments, all his pleas and justifications, come to nothing in the face of this declaration. This is the way it is and even if she had the will to change it, it couldn't be done. Her only suggestion is that he find himself another outlet.

'Are you,' he says, 'suggesting I go to prostitutes?'

'It doesn't have to be as sordid as that. You could find someone for yourself. A fuck buddy, I think they're called.'

'That's a term for teenagers,' is all he can say. He is momentarily thrown by her casual use of this scatology, for her distaste for the act itself has long begotten a distaste for the coarser ways of referencing it.

She just shrugs. 'Well, you know what I mean,' she says, and that is the end of the conversation.

All Maurice's subsequent attempts to elaborate on this revelation come to nothing. It is something she just doesn't care to talk about.

Up on the deck with their sandwiches, they sit on their newly purchased sunloungers and attempt their first civil conversation since he brought home the rabbit a couple of days before. Their talk is desultory, almost the talk of strangers. This is how it always is when they are emerging from a day or two of silence, their subsequent interactions forming not so much conversation as entries plucked blindly from a drawerful of vapidities and presented to a cold void in which the conditions for nurturing life are almost absent. They talk of their plans for the rest of the day (her – a visit to the salon to have her nails done, a meeting in a café with two other mothers to plan a petition for their son's school, food shopping, making the dinner; him – reading the papers), her level of satisfaction with the latest round of house renovations (generally low on account of the joins in the skirting boards, the replacement of which he has not even noticed), and the dim possibility of his taking a job that would involve a lot of travel (a prospect on which she maintains an admirable uninterest). Their altercation over the rabbit still hangs between them, fracturing the flow of every sentence as they seek a topic that is neutral and interesting enough to carry them to some sort of restoration. Beneath them, in a shaded corner of the yard under the eaves of the garden shed, is the hutch. Is it Maurice's imagination or does he catch a faint whiff of soggy rabbit compost on the air?

'Maybe I should go and get a new bale of straw this afternoon,' Maurice ventures. He does not intend this to stir, he mentions it merely as an opportunity to put the matter to rest.

She says nothing, just gives him the single grave nod which is her habit when she has decided not to take his bait. They finish their sandwiches in silence.

Now his wife is gathering up the empty plates. Maurice will long remember that she stands for a moment in front of the sun which, despite a cooling breeze, has been nicely warming his bare legs. Suddenly he is cold.

'Maurice,' she says. 'There's something I have to say to you. I don't want you to interrupt me. I don't want you to say a word. I just want you to listen to what I have to say and we can discuss what needs to be discussed some other time.'

She glances briefly into the distant valley before continuing. When she says the words, Maurice somehow feels he has already heard them.

'I don't want to share this house with you any more. I want you to move out. I've been thinking about this for some time and this is the decision I've come to. I just do not want to be married to you any more. It's not going to change. I'm not going to change my mind.'

By now, he is hardly listening. Although it is the last thing he has been expecting, he finds that the only surprise about her message is the unbending resolve with which it is delivered. It must have been well re-hearsed. It is only when, possibly flustered at his reaction, she begins to ad lib, that she stumbles. There is no point fighting her for the house, she says. As the primary carer, there is no question of her not staying here with their son. Any court would agree. Of course, it goes without saying that he can see him as often as he wants. If, that is, he does want. She drops the used cutlery on the plates and walks back into the house. Is it Maurice's imagination or does she tauten her stride in such a way that there is no lilt to her behind inside her tennis skirt?

He sits there for a moment, attempting to gather about himself an appropriate sense of occasion. All he can really think is that his legs felt cold when she stood in front of the sun. He is not surprised, but he is still shocked. Life is comfortable for his wife. She has all the things she wants: a nice big house with the freedom to do with it more or less as she pleases, the ability to parade as a devoted parent for the smallest poss-ible price, days free of deadlines and difficult colleagues and the general pressures of making a living, days she can shape as she pleases. Even if their marriage lacks the fire that had burned at its outset, he feels it has settled into a level of mutual tolerance that suits them both. Her de-pendence on him, he is sure, is such that she would never dare rock the boat for fear of risking these things, and it encourages him to a wider and wider leeway in his own behaviour. Sometimes he has believed he could get away with anything. Now here she is, asserting in a well-honed speech that it is over. Maurice doesn't believe it for a moment.

That afternoon, he decides to go for a drive, ostensibly in search of that straw bale. This takes him to the northern edge of the city, where the first few acres of farmland meet the final suburbs. Afterwards, he continues driving, along the old highway. Before the motorway was built, this was the main route north; now it is a sort of ghost road, where solitary vehicles can have its expanse of well-maintained bitumen more or less to themselves. Here and there are fruit stalls and old-fashioned petrol stations, most long since abandoned but one or two still open for whatever paltry business they can conjure up. He drives with pleasure, enjoying the quiet perfection of the engine as he moves between the gears, the responsiveness of the pedals beneath his feet, the simple power and control at his disposal. When his fingers are not caressing the gearstick, his hand rests on the soft cream leather of the passenger seat, where once he might have encountered his wife's thigh.

His first impulse is to take her on, to challenge her right to remain in the house. Any other approach, it seems, would be a backward step, and he is not a man to take a backward step. In his career, he knows that to beat his rivals, to take the prizes, he has to look only to his own interests and the most effective means of serving them. In this way, he has found it relatively easy to progress and has never – until the past few months of course – been impeded on his path.

Perhaps recent events have made him wary, perhaps that solitary drive along the old highway has had a mellowing effect, perhaps it is the sudden realisation that he has the means to confound her – whatever it is, he decides then and there not to engage in that battle. This is his wife. It is not the same as his work. It never has been. He will not go head to head with her. He will phone his sisters and persuade them to delay the auction for a few months (if necessary citing some economic data predicting an imminent rise in house prices), and he will move, with bewildering speed and a revelatory lack of fuss, into Aunt Patricia's house. That is what he will do. He will be gone before the weekend. She will hardly know what has hit her.

The road is wide and inviting, and there have not yet been enough years since the advent of the motorway for the neglect to show on the road surface. He puts his foot down, confident in the unlikelihood of being caught.

*

Things move quickly after this, more quickly than any of them would have believed possible. That same evening, having spoken with his sisters, he is in a position to inform his wife that he will be moving at the weekend. As he tells her, he watches her closely. He imagines that she will be startled by the speed of his movements. She might even be awed. He is looking for a trace of the way she used to look at him, that mixture of pride and admiration, when she saw him as the person who could fix what was wrong in her world. But she knows he is studying her and betrays nothing.

Assuming, not incorrectly, that his behaviour is part of a hidden plan, she remains as hard as iron over the next few days, even going through their possessions, room by room, cupboard by cupboard, drawer by drawer, and arranging in the garage those items she is prepared to cede to him or that she considers to have belonged to him in the first place.

During this time, they have no conversations not directly related to the practicalities of moving, the things he will need to maintain his own household, the things it already has. It is a game of brinkmanship, it seems, as each waits for the other to crack. Nothing is said about the custody of their son who, perhaps encouraged by his father's assurance that the split is only temporary, refuses to take the situation seriously. Nothing is said about the financial arrangements either. In his own re-flections on the subject, the main difficulty, and the factor that seems most likely to, as it were, bring her to her senses, is the cost of running two households. After all the renovations, the mortgage on the house is still hefty and, buoyed by his many successes, she has never been frugal about maintaining it. As a family, they have always lived at the edge of their means. Sometimes she has even pushed them further, in confidence that they will catch up with his next pay rise, or bonus, or redundancy package – her blind faith in the ever upward trajectory of his career. But she has always baulked at expenses from which she can see no direct ad-vantage. He wonders whether she has finally seen the proposed benefits of his moving out as being worth the extra costs involved. In any case, he thinks, her reasoning must include consideration of all the extra money he will now have to earn. Since he is not currently earning any, it shows a touching faith in his capacity to do so, a faith he has done no-thing to diminish.

Maurice moves out just after yellow sticker day. The removalists come that Monday morning, in the modest-sized van he has ordered. As he surveys his little haul, clustered in one corner of their exuberantly proportioned garage, he feels something he has never expected to feel, a curious lightening of the heart, an unburdening commensurate with the weight of things being no longer his responsibility. He makes all the right noises, expresses all the expected resentment at the furniture, the ornaments, the household appliances she has earmarked for herself, listens to the different justifications she has prepared, but the truth, hardly acknowledged by himself, is that every item that stays with her represents a load removed from his shoulders. It is a feeling he would never have foreseen.

5

Maurice never went to university. In his opinion, it was a waste of time, a pointless deferral of life and its real business. It is a decision he has never had cause to regret. He saw friends who did go living in semi-squalor with other students, sometimes even sharing a bedroom, having endless arguments over money and parties and washing-up, scratching around for the price of a drink while he had his own unit, with a new car and money to spend. Inevitably, those people are no longer his friends. One of them lived, for a time, a few streets away from Patricia's house, so he has known the area slightly for a number of years. It is still full of students and, as he sees it, other assorted lowlife, as well as a smattering of professional types, presumably attracted to the area's rakish charm, who have been buying up and renovating the old terraces.

On moving in here, there are two things he notices right away – the number of people out and about and the difficulty of parking his car. Up where he now lives, the only people ever about are joggers and dog walkers. (At different times, for short periods, he has been both – the only reasons he has ever had for actually setting foot on the ground outside his front gate.) Down here, it is hard to walk far on any footpath without having to step aside for someone. And yes, he has started walking – much of the time it is the only way to get to where he wants to go. Parking spots are so precious that he is loath to give one up for a journey that could be made by some other means. Sometimes, he has even found himself taking a bus. Maurice has never been one for public transport. As a young man, he once heard it said that catching the bus to work after the age of thirty is a mark of failure. It is a dictum to which he has enthusiastically subscribed ever since in his quest to avoid mixing with the hoi polloi. Even from his office, he used to like descending to the street with an entourage, lest he be mistaken for one of them. Now look at him.

During these first few days in his new home, he does a lot of walking. It is perfect autumn weather, with days full of sunshine and temperatures in the low twenties. As he walks, it seems he is being introduced to another world, a world of whose existence he has only been dimly aware. At first, he wonders whether anybody around here actually works. There are people all over the place and no one looks anything like the office workers in the city only a mile or two away. Nobody looks productive at all. There are men about his age going around in T-shirts and jeans, there are grey-haired women with militant airs and mad-looking clothes, there are beggars and charity collectors and pamphleteers clogging up the footpaths, there are people carrying books in the street, or musical instruments, there are youngsters with their tattoos and piercings and bravado, all somehow alike in their striving to be unique. There are also always a few of the drunk and the deranged laying claim to the public benches or the tables outside cafés, and then there are the old and incapacitated gamely getting about with sticks or walking frames or, most commonly, motorised scooters. The obvious answer to his question is that most of these people don't work, or if they do they have jobs that don't stop them frequenting cafés all day. Some of them, he thinks, must be artists or agitators of some kind, probably criminals too. For years, he has been living a sealed existence between his home, his car and his offices in the city. If he had ever given it any thought, which he has not, he would have imagined all suburbs to be much the same as his, quite unlike the teeming world that awaits him every time he opens his new front door. It is really quite invigorating, he finds.

*

The first person he invites to visit him at his new home is the woman his wife so unexpectedly referred to as his fuck buddy. She is a corporate

60

lawyer, an advisor, if not a partner, to his ill-fated investment scheme. They have been sleeping together intermittently for a year, most of their assignations taking place in hotel rooms in the city. Although they were actually fuck buddies before he heard his wife use the term, Maurice sticks to the notion that he has never cheated on her because the relationship now has her blessing. He told her about it, just a few weeks after she had made her suggestion, thus attaining the twin satisfactions of reassurance at his honesty and surprising her over the speed with which he had been able to find someone. She said nothing at the time and remained silent, completely silent, for three days. When she finally decided to talk, he reminded her of her suggestion. She couldn't have it both ways, he said. At first she claimed the suggestion had not been serious. But, finally admitting that it had been at the time, she insisted it was a spur of the moment remark around which she had expected some discussion before he rushed off to put it into practice. He shrugged. Even now, he shrugs. He rather fancies this view of himself as a dangerous dog, unleashed at her peril. In any case, he said, what on earth was there to discuss? She had said the only thing that needed to be said. She countered with the accusation that as long as he was able to logically justify his side of the argument, he always believed there was nothing more to be said. Maurice accepted the truth of this, but he still believed his view to be correct. In the end, though, he stated something which was also the truth, that he would rather be making love to her.

The way they are dressed, on this evening of a working day, immediately attests to the divergence in their lives. His buddy, his friend, is wearing her dark blue, pinstriped business suit, black stockings and a knee-length skirt. Maurice wears blue jeans and a green polo shirt. She has never seen him dressed this way, while he has never known her to wear anything else. Her blouse, across the chest, is finished with a sort of ruff, whose feathery ripples find an echo in the curls of her hair. It speaks of a serious woman who is not above indulging some frivolity from time to time. Maurice's immediate thought is to restore equality between them by helping her out of the suit. This has, after all, been the pattern of their previous couplings, mostly characterised by an urgency that has seen them lunge at one another as soon as the hotel door is closed, in the knowledge that he has to get back home before the evening is out. It is an urgency that has become ritualised to the point where it is hard for him to see them proceeding in any other way. This, however, is the first time they have met on either of their home turfs, so to speak, and the rules are necessarily different. Even though he has hardly established this place as his own, it is not neutral ground. For the first time, it occurs to him that this relationship might be heading into new territory, that besides her body and her business mind he hardly knows this woman at all. For instance, he does not know whether she has parents still alive, where she went to school or the names of her siblings, and he can be pretty sure she does not know those things about him.

He makes them drinks – a pale ale for him, an iceless gin and tonic for her with a sliver of lime bought especially for the purpose that afternoon (this is something he does know about her, her choice of drink – he also knows that she likes a well oiled finger inserted into her anus during intercourse), and they sit together in Aunt Patricia's living room and think of things to say to each other. The two parts of the room, which take up most of the house's ground floor, are divided by an archway that might once have concealed sliding doors. As is usually the case with these terraces, the rooms are quarantined from both the front door and the stairs by a narrow hallway that leads straight to a smaller archway beyond which lies the kitchen. They sit on either end of Aunt Patricia's unexpectedly well proportioned couch, under the big arch, facing back towards the front windows. Behind them is a dining table with six matching chairs, another new acquisition since the time of his grandmother and already earmarked by his sister, and before them, in a corner next to the window, the large TV screen looms from its perch on what appears to be a packing case. There is nothing else between them and the window except a small coffee table, from which he has already removed an assortment of magazines, and a pair of mismatched dining chairs she had been apportioned on the death of her sister. Maurice's own house is three, possibly four times the size of this one, yet here it is possible to feel quite overwhelmed by the amount of space. He supposes it is because so much of it is unused here, devoid of the sort of clutter usually to be found in these houses. He wonders how a figure as frail and insignificant as Aunt Patricia managed to inhabit this place at all.

Maurice had been looking forward to this night. It would be their first time away from the furtive neutrality of a hotel room. (It would also be his first opportunity to thoroughly revel in his wife's mistake.) Now, however, it becomes apparent that the two of them do not have a lot to talk about. Up to now, any time together not spent in bed has been spent discussing the scheme. Even in their brief post-coital moments, it has become a sort of default subject to which they inevitably return after more than a few minutes on anything else. He stretches out his legs to try to establish some sense of ease. The evening spreads out in front of them. Lust might still save them, as it normally does, but they now seem to have this unspoken agreement to prove their relationship in another dimension first. Suddenly he is worrying about waking up with her tomorrow morning. Perhaps her thoughts have been running along similar lines for, after establishing that he is not in any position to cook them a satisfactory meal, she suggests they go out to eat. He seizes on the proposal.

The Thai restaurant where they find themselves some ten minutes later seems more conducive to the cosy intimacy they are seeking than the expanses of Aunt Patricia's living room. Their talk begins to flow and when it lapses, as it inevitably does, back to business, neither of them makes any attempt to steer it away. It is, after all, the one thing they know they have in common and a subject on which they have already proved they can converse for hours. As they sink deeper into their discussion in their little booth, under the benevolent eyes of half a dozen glowing Buddhas, it occurs to Maurice that it is enough to know the things he does know about this woman and that there is no particular need to look for anything else. It would, surely, be a mistake to look for a new dimension in this relationship when he is already getting from it the only thing he really wants.

With this realisation, he regards her across the table, studiously twisting noodles onto her chopsticks, earrings dangling amongst corkscrew curls, and he feels a surge of benevolence towards her. Slowly he finds her leg under the table and rubs it with his foot. His only thought is to pay the bill and get her back to the house as soon as possible. He even thinks about booking them a room in a hotel by way of celebration.

She does not look up. 'Tell me something, Maurice,' she says. 'Are you interested in me at all?'

'What do you mean?' he says. 'Of course I am.'

She continues, as though he has not replied. 'You never ask me anything about myself.' She is still slowly twisting the noodles but now her earrings are still, no longer catching the light from the Buddhas.

Maurice thinks quickly. What she is saying is probably true, but then the same might be said of her. He says so.

'But that just isn't the case, Maurice. You just won't talk about yourself. Whenever I ask you anything personal, anything that's not about sex, you refuse to be drawn. You give me that grunt of yours.'

Maurice's response to this, no doubt, would be interpreted as a grunt. She is not finished. This time she swallows a noodle, rests both elbows on the table and looks at him across the backs of her layered hands. It is a look that might be used to unnerve a courtroom witness.

'Tell me,' she says, 'what do you want from this relationship?' Then, without giving him the chance to gather his thoughts, 'When you invited me to your home this evening, what was your intention?'

'Well…' he shrugs.

'Were you intending for me to stay the night?'

Maurice says something about seeing how it went.

'Because if you were, then we were going to need something to talk about in the morning.'

How can Maurice tell her that these have been his own thoughts? How could he say anything at all without jeopardising his chance of a fuck? For that, it's now clear, is all he does want.

He calls for the bill only to be informed, via the waiter's curt backwards jerk of the head, that he is expected to pay at the counter. This is not the sort of establishment he is used to.

'How,' she says, 'can I be involved with a man who gives so little of himself?'

Maurice sees his chance receding. Maybe there is nothing more to be said, nothing more to be done but walk her back to her car and see her on her way.

The walk back takes them along the bright main street for a few minutes, past a crossing with traffic lights, then down the more dimly lighted road where he now lives. As they wait at the lights, a bent old woman in a mac comes by, pushing a shopping trolley with greasy plastic bags hung around its edges like fenders. Her smell suddenly overwhelms them, a stench so strong it is a wonder she can stand it herself. She has three dogs in tow, an Alsatian and two small terriers. They follow her quietly and obediently, just as any dogs would follow their owner. It strikes Maurice that dogs take no notice of the status of their mistress or master, fawning regardless.

They walk on up the slight incline after the traffic lights, neither of them talking, separated by a yard or so of space. Because she is wearing heels, he has to slow to half his normal walking pace, and the sound of her shoes on the footpath demotes all the other street noises to the background. They turn into his road where, as usual, there are parked cars nose to tail on either side. Soft street lighting is widely spaced here, which means a few steps of darkness between the orbit of one lamp and the next. In front of Aunt Patricia's house, a small hedge has been allowed to grow, blocking the view of the front door from the street.

'Did you leave the lights on?' she says.

'Just the hall light,' Maurice says. 'I always leave something on. There are a lot of burglaries around here.'

'What about upstairs?'

He steps back and looks up at the bedroom, behind the balcony's cast-iron railings. At the side from which they have approached, it had been obscured by a tree. Sure enough, the lights up there are blazing.

Dusk had been falling as they left the house, and it had been broad day-light when he had last been in that room, which meant either the lights must have been left on all day or someone had turned them on while they've been out. He checks the number on the little gate to make sure this is the right house.

'There's someone in there,' she says in a low voice.

They go back to the footpath for a better view. Behind the glass on the balcony doors, behind the flimsy curtains, someone is moving. It is immediately obvious that they are taking their time. They are not rush-ing from one place to another, one repository of potential loot to the next, as he imagines a real burglar would, but then he imagines a real burglar would not operate with the lights on. This person is moving about at leisure, as though they have a right to be here. The only people Maurice can think of who might feel this way are his sisters and his son. None of them has a key. In any case, his sisters would never have poked around like this in what is now his bedroom, and his son, in the unlikely event of his deciding to pay Maurice a visit, would undoubtedly have sprawled himself in front of the TV if he had somehow managed to break in.

'You weren't expecting someone, were you?' she says, a little frostily this time.

He shakes his head. His receding hopes return for a moment. Per-haps gallantry of some sort will save the day.

They watch for a few more seconds. The light in the bedroom goes out. Maurice strides towards the door.

'What are you doing?' she hisses.

'I'm going to see what's going on.' Thwarted lust is making him reck-less. He wants to confront this intruder. He happens to know that his golf clubs are standing just inside the front door and he has already de-cided which one he is going to use.

'Don't be stupid!' She directs him back onto the footpath, with a furious motion of her hand. 'Call the police,' she says. Then, when he hesitates, 'If you don't, I will.'

He thinks for a moment, then shrugs and walks towards her. They retreat further, to the other side of the road, and from behind a parked VW van he dials the emergency number for the first time in his life. There is no point arguing with her. She is a lawyer, after all.

It must be a quiet evening for crime in their suburb, for the police arrive in minutes. There are three of them, all alarmingly young-looking, their eyes hardened by a professional crust of insouciance. Maurice makes himself known to them as they cruise past. Without leaving the car, the driver dangles a bare arm down the outside of his door and asks the preliminary questions. Maurice describes how they had been about to enter the house when they noticed the figure moving in the upstairs bedroom.

'And where had you been, sir?' the driver asks, somewhat irrelevantly, it seems to Maurice.

Nevertheless, he describes their visit to the restaurant, the time they left and the time they returned.

'And this,' the policeman nods in the direction of his friend, who has so far kept out of the conversation, 'is your wife?'

'This is a friend of mine.'

The policeman nods slowly, with an air of insolence, it seems to Maurice. He looks over to the house, across the front of his colleague in the passenger seat, who looks over as well.

'There's no light on now,' he says.

'I told you, they turned it off.'

'And no one has left the house?'

'Not from the front.'

'What about the back?'

'I don't know, I can't see through to the back from here.'

Again, the policeman nods slowly. It is hard to tell whether he is doing this because he needs the time to digest Maurice's answers or because this is his way of establishing the upper hand. 'Any sign of a break in, sir?'

'Not from the front.'

'What about the back?'

'I told you. I haven't been round the back.'

'Was anyone else in the house with you, sir, before you went out?'

Maurice no longer believes he is asking these questions in good faith. Even the word 'sir', on his lips, seems laced with irony.

'Listen,' he says, 'I called you because I saw an intruder in my house. Everything else is immaterial. Just do your job and make sure it's safe for me to open my own front door.' Maurice has the satisfaction of seeing a quick look of surprise cross the policeman's face.

When the policeman speaks again, his tone of voice is markedly more businesslike. 'Just one more question, sir, if you don't mind,' he says. 'Does anyone else have a key to the house?'

Maurice thinks of his sisters, whom he has already discounted as possible visitors. 'No,' he says firmly.

The policeman nods. 'Wait here.' He drives forwards a little way and turns into a nearby side street.

All three of them now leave the car and walk back towards Maurice. One of them gestures to him as they approach the house. From their belts dangle numerous heavy objects; baton, torch, radio, keys and of course, on the hip, in its holster, the gun, looking surprisingly slight for an object of such potential. Maurice follows with his key, feeling slightly exposed.

'Is there a way round the back?' the first policeman asks him quietly as they approach the front door.

Maurice points to the side passage, behind the two sentinel-like garbage bins, and with a snap of the fingers the policeman dispatches one of his colleagues. Now it is the three of them standing at the front door. His other colleague cups his face up against the door's glass panel.

After a few seconds, he turns away. 'Nothing,' he says, less quietly than seems wise. He speaks as though this is the definitive verdict, as though Maurice, as suspected, has been proved wrong.

'I didn't call you out for fun,' Maurice says. He puts his own face up to the panel. The interior glows in a dim yellow haze behind the coloured glass. Maurice recalls switching off the kitchen light before they left, yet it now seems to be on. He says this to the first policeman, who shrugs.

'Would you mind unlocking the door, sir,' the policeman says, 'then just wait out here for me.'

Maurice does as he is asked, pulling the key back a fraction towards himself before turning it, a trick he discovered on his first night here when for several minutes he had wondered whether he was ever going to find his way in. They walk past him into the hall. As the first one disappears around the corner into the lounge room, Maurice is gratified to see him place a hand on his gun. But when he draws it, it is only his torch.

In the road behind him, a low-slung car snakes past, a beatbox thumping inside at a level that seems to hold the entire atmosphere in its thrall. Maurice looks for his friend near the VW. She is standing where he left her, watching the proceedings. Through the front window, he can now see the odd splash of light as the police shine their torches around the house. Finally they switch on the main light and he hears them heading up the stairs, whose peculiar creaking has already become familiar to him, again less quietly than seems wise.

While he waits for them, Maurice stands on the footpath and surveys the street that is now his home, with its parked cars mirroring the cluttered arrangements of the houses themselves, its tired but valiant trees, its distant rumble of traffic noise, its vague smell of uncollected garbage, its myriad sources of light. He is struck, as he has not been before, by the contrast with where he lived before, where cars are all kept in garages or driveways leaving the streets wide and empty, where big houses brood in silence among lush and abundant foliage that always smells as sweet as after a rain shower, where the police are polite and deferential, if seen at all, and where the distant freeway can only be heard when the air drifts from a certain direction. Here, you can hear life from all sides, whether it is the traffic noise, the shouts of revellers or the ebb and flow of music from cars and open windows. A hundred yards away, shining in its own unearthly glow, is the main street with its bars and eating places, and at the end of that street is the thoroughfare that leads to the city centre where traffic flows like blood in an artery, carrying the stream of nourishment that keeps it alive at all hours. Even though the police are scouring his house for an intruder, he hardly dares move his car, and his wife and son are sleeping in what might as well be another country, he is starting to feel a part of this world, as he has not done before now.

Across the road, his friend is now walking back and forth, with her phone against her head. She does not seem to be talking, only listening. He waves, and she nods without moving the phone. Then there is a noise from the house.

The door is half open how and he can see right through to the foot of the stairs. He hears a series of dull thumps, then the familiar creaking of the floorboards but in the wrong order. More thumps, quick barked commands, then three figures wrestle their way to the bottom of the stairs. The second figure is handcuffing the first and together with the third is pushing him out of the door but not before this second figure, the policeman who did all the earlier talking, places a seemingly friendly hand behind the first figure's neck and drives his forehead into the edge of the open door. It looks like a quite deliberate attempt to injure him, which Maurice would not have seen if he had been standing anywhere else. It both shocks and excites him. The handcuffed man staggers forwards, but is prevented from falling by the other policeman. He emerges into the light from the porch, face pointing at the ground, still being jostled along, still staggering, still prevented from falling. The first of him Maurice clearly sees is his shiny helmet of lead-grey hair, all with a remarkable ability to remain in place in spite of what is happening to him. Under the light, he finally looks up. A wispy delta of blood claws the left side of his face.

Maurice recognises Sandford at once. The blood seems to suit him, as though it is the final touch required for his face to reveal its true character. Sandford speaks Maurice's name. The policeman loosens his grip. Sandford stands up straight.

'What the hell do you think you're doing here?' Maurice says.

'What are you doing here?' Sandford counters.

'What's going on?' says the policeman. 'Do you know each other?'

'I know who this is,' says Maurice.

'So whose house is this?'

'It's mine,' says Maurice. 'It's where I live.'

'What about him?'

'He doesn't live here.'

Sandford says nothing. Blood is now dripping from his face but disappears into the grey carpet.

'But he's a friend of yours, is he?'

'He's known to me, that's all.'

'Thanks, Maurice,' says Sandford.

The policeman fixes Maurice with a sceptical eye.

'I've met him once before,' says Maurice. 'What are you going to do with him?'

'We'll arrest him for burglary,' he says, 'if that's what you want.'

'I haven't stolen anything!' says Sandford.

'Trespass then.'

'I'm not trespassing!'

'Why did you break in then?' says the other policeman.

'I didn't,' he says. 'I came in through the front door.' He dips a hand into one of his back pockets, an awkward manoeuvre as it is handcuffed to the other one. He retrieves something with two fingers but he is unable to show them what it is because he cannot bring either hand around to the front of his body, so he drops it onto the brick path.

It is a key. The other policeman picks it up. No key ring, metallic red and well worn. He gives it to the first one, who presents it, on an open palm, to Maurice.

'We'll leave him with you then, shall we,' he says, '…sir?'

**6**

'You did the right thing, Maurice,' says Sandford. 'You're one of the good guys.'

'Never mind that,' Maurice says. 'You'd better go and clean yourself up. I take it you know where the bathroom is.'

Sandford nods. He is holding a handkerchief to his cut, so he is no longer dripping blood onto the paving stones.

While he climbs the stairs, Maurice goes out to look for his friend. Even now, his thought is that once Sandford has cleaned himself up, he can be packed off and they can resume their evening. Apart from anything else, her presence will give him an excuse to get rid of Sandford, who has shown no intention to leave.

The VW is still there but she is missing. As he crosses the road, he notices tail lights weaving away from him between the two lines of parked cars. He hardly noticed her car when she arrived, beyond a vague recognition that it was small and dark in colour, possibly green. The car he is watching now is dark, and fits easily into the narrow space available to it. He stands there and gives a slow, full wave. It continues on its way, slowly putting distance between them. He walks along to the side street where she parked, the same one in which the police stopped their car. Someone is already reversing into her vacated space.

Back in the house, Sandford calls out to him. Maurice goes upstairs to find him stooped over the basin, which is ringed with several lines of pink. Like everything else in the bathroom, the basin is old, and he envisages Sandford's blood permanently staining the worn enamel.

'Have you got some plaster?' he says.

Maurice does not, but he has a box of tissues from which he plucks him five or six.

'That's good, Maurice,' he says, as though Maurice has displayed un-warranted generosity by giving him so many. He has not managed to staunch the blood flow, and he is making so much mess that Maurice has to help him.

The cut, just above his eyebrow, is a good two inches long and little gouts of blood still throb from the wound. It looks as though he needs stitches, but Maurice has no intention of extending their acquaintance by driving him to the nearby hospital. (The last time he did this, with his son after a rugby smash-up, it took them four hours to be seen.) The only benefit of stitches would be to reduce the size of Sandford's scar, which is no concern of Maurice's.

He folds some of the tissues into a pad and presses it to Sandford's forehead. Sandford does not seem to understand his instructions to keep the pressure sustained and Maurice has to take his tobacco-yellowed fingers in his own to guide them into place. (For the rest of the night, he will smell the nicotine on his hand.) As he does this, he becomes conscious of Sandford's breathing, and the physical closeness he should have been sharing with someone else. Sandford's breath has a faecal smoker's smell. Maurice cleans blood from his face with water-soaked tissues. From here, he is able to appraise Sandford's facial quirks – another scar, obviously stitched, along his jawline, short blond hairs sprouting from the tip of his nose, shadowed areas in his cheeks where facial hair clusters – in a way he has never done with another man.

Sandford's grey eyes appraise him briefly in return, seeming to look both through and beyond him. 'You're doing the right thing, Maurice,' he says again, as Maurice leaves him to it, with an admonishment to wipe around the basin with toilet paper and throw the used tissues into the bowl.

Somehow he finds it necessary to tell Sandford to do things that would be obvious to anyone else. 'And while you're doing that,' he says, recognising the hint of blackmail in Sandford's constant professions of appreciation, 'you can think of a reason why I shouldn't take you back to the police and have you charged.'

Sandford stays in the bathroom for a long time, it seems – a good half hour. Maurice keeps listening up the stairs to make sure he has not escaped out of an upstairs window. Every now and then, he hears the toilet flushing, or a quiet clanking from the pipes in the kitchen which means the taps are being run.

Eventually, Sandford comes down, holding a clean pad of tissues to his head. He descends the stairs very slowly, as though he does not fully trust his legs. He has a headache, he says. Maurice offers to get him a pill. Thanks, he says. Maurice goes up to the bathroom and picks out something from his hastily assembled medicine cabinet. There seem to be fewer pills left in the packet than he remembers, but Sandford claims not to have touched them. Now Maurice is going to the sink and filling a glass, an action Sandford could perform perfectly well for himself. What concern is it of his, he thinks, if he wants to overdo the dosage? What concern is any of this of his?

Evidently, Sandford has been rehearsing his response to Maurice's earlier question, for this is what he now provides. The substance of his argument is that he is entitled to be here because of Patricia. According to Sandford, she wanted him to have the house.

'But it wasn't hers,' Maurice says. 'She couldn't leave it to you.'

'It was her home,' Sandford says, as though it is a relevant assertion.

'It may have been her home, but it belonged to me and my sisters. Patricia was only allowed to stay here under the terms of our grandmother's will. In no sense did she own it.'

Sandford stares at Maurice with his good eye, as though attempting to make sense of what he is saying. His other hand is still holding the pad of tissues up to his forehead. But at least the bleeding seems to have stopped. His head seems bigger. Perhaps there is some swelling under the hairline. Maurice has found some electrical tape, which he offers him, in lieu of plaster, to hold the pad in place. They go into the kitchen to look for scissors. Maurice does not offer to help this time. He has no desire to further his acquaintance with the landscape of Sandford's face.

Sandford takes the tape and the scissors and sets about finding the free end with his bulbous, well-chewed finger ends, rubbing away to no avail while Maurice resists the temptation to snatch it back and do it for him. He suggests using the scissors to expose the tape's end, which he does, thanking Maurice again as though the thought would never have occurred to him. He cuts a couple of lengths, far too short, and presses them blindly up against the pad. Most of it doesn't adhere. The pad hangs like a blinker on a horse.

Maurice can stand it no longer. 'Here,' he says. He takes the tape and the scissors, cuts off three or four lengths and attaches them himself, this time staying at arm's length.

Sandford seems unable to keep his head still and the job is far from neat, but he does not care and he does not seem to notice Maurice's distaste.

When he has finished, Sandford says to him, 'I want a cup of tea, Maurice.'

With his peculiar way of expressing himself, he has managed to state this neither as a request nor a command, but as a statement that allows for no contradiction. Maurice finds himself boiling the kettle and dropping the tea bags into the mugs. Remembering the tea they drank in his room, he even takes down the sugar from its place in the cupboard. Meanwhile, Sandford has produced his smoking materials and is rolling himself a cigarette. He has the paper spread flat across one hand and sprinkles it with tobacco from the other. He seems to be on autopilot now, and his fingers go about their business with nimble habituation. It is fascinating to watch their transformation in the face of this familiar task. With quick, efficient movements, he has soon fashioned something he can smoke. He starts to light up.

'I'd rather you didn't smoke in the house,' Maurice says.

Almost imperceptibly, but to Maurice's satisfaction, Sandford straightens his back and in his posture an unguarded nuance assumes itself which, if it does not directly say so, at least allows for the possibility of subjugation. He tells Maurice he wants to stay inside.

In that case, don't light it, Maurice tells him.

Sandford stops and looks at Maurice, cigarette between lips, hand cupped, lighter poised.

Maurice will not now be defied. 'If you want to smoke,' he says, 'I want you to go outside. I don't want smoking in this…in my house.'

Sandford uncups his hand, repockets the lighter. Maurice nods. Now he finds himself carrying the two mugs outside, to the bench next to the porch where Patricia always used to be waiting when he arrived to pick her up. They both sit down and Sandford lights his cigarette. Now Maurice has to consume his smoke just as much as if they had been in the house. There is a crisp aroma about Sandford's tobacco which he finds not unpleasant. It reminds him of his own brief time as a schoolboy smoker. Sandford sucks in hard and sighs.

'So, are you going to tell me what you were doing here?' Maurice says.

'Sure, Maurice. I came for my things.'

'What things?'

'I had it all stored up in the bedroom. It's not there any more.'

'I don't know what you're talking about,' Maurice says, hoping Sandford does not notice the brief tremor of artifice in his voice.

Sandford explains further, describing some of the items, the bicycles, the phones. It was all worth money to him, he says. The bike Maurice has commandeered for his son still stands outside the back door, waiting for his mother to drive down and pick it up in the Landcruiser. Maurice decides to deny all knowledge should Sandford find it, just as he has denied all knowledge of the rest of his things. He has no idea how Sandford might react if he told him the truth. It seems simpler to play dumb, safer too.

'Someone must have come in and taken it all,' Sandford says. He does not seem to find this particularly surprising, although he does mention, again, that it would have been worth a lot of money to him.

'It must have happened before I moved in,' says Maurice, not untruthfully. 'Are you sure you had things stored here?' He is pleased to note no tremor in his voice this time.

Sandford stares at him for a second. The tape is starting to come away from his skin. Although mercifully black, and not green or red, it still looks absurd, like a huge spider clinging to his brow. It makes the sudden menace in his stare all the more palpable.

'Are you calling me a liar, Maurice?' he says. 'Because I'm telling you the truth. How am I supposed to live? Most of it didn't even belong to me.'

'Who did it belong to?' Maurice says, hoping to move the subject away from lying.

'It belonged to different people,' he says. 'Patricia had a lot of space she didn't need. We used to keep stuff here for people. They paid us for it. Good money. They won't be happy about this.'

'Who are these people?' says Maurice.

'I can't tell you that.'

'What are they going to do when they find it's missing?'

'I don't know. But they won't be happy.'

'So you've said. I'm just wondering how they're going to demonstrate this unhappiness.'

'How should I know that, Maurice?' The sudden sharpness in his voice is a direct rebuttal of Maurice's sarcasm. It is unnerving and Maurice finds himself backing away.

'I'm sorry,' he says, 'I was just wondering if there was anyone else with a key to this house.'

They are back inside now, in the kitchen, nursing their half-drunk mugs of tea. It is a large room, with a floor of red linoleum and cupboards and bench tops which must have been installed at different times. Maurice's wife would have refused even to boil a kettle in here.

Now Sandford asks Maurice about his rabbit. Maurice tells him it is at the other house, with his son.

'I thought you were going to look after it, Maurice.'

'What made you think that?'

'It was in my note.'

'So it was. But I was under no obligation to take it. You should have asked me. Anyway, it's perfectly all right.'

'You said you used to have one.'

'That's neither here nor there. It didn't mean I was offering to look after the damned thing.'

Sandford doesn't say anything, he merely looks puzzled. Again there is a hiatus, one of those peculiar conversational gaps which seems to show Sandford holding all the cards.

Maurice's only idea is to fill it. 'Anyway,' he says, 'what on earth was that about?'

'What?'

'Your disappearing act. I mean, why did you go away?'

Sandford ponders for a moment before answering. 'I didn't think I wanted to be part of this,' he says eventually.

'I beg your pardon?'

'This.' With an economical gesture, he indicates the room, the house, the world.

'So you went away?'

'Yes.'

'But you came back.'

'Yes.'

'Why?'

'Why what?'

'Why did you go away? Why did you come back?'

Sandford does not seem keen to expand. There is another pause, a long one this time. Maurice wonders why he is asking these questions. He is well aware that they will only delay the moment when he can get Sandford out of his house – out of his life – but there are things he wants to know, he finds, and the only way he might get answers is by asking. He carefully changes tack and manages to extract from him the story of how he has come to be in the house.

By the time he has finished his explanation, Maurice is convinced he is telling the truth and that he was unaware anyone was actually living here. Either he is remarkably unobservant or Maurice is travelling more lightly than he'd imagined and his belongings have made little impression on the general state of the house. As far as Sandford is concerned, he is exercising his right, inferred from his possession of a key, to come in and check on his things. He tells Maurice how the police roughed him up in the bedroom before bringing him downstairs, but in a way that is matter of fact and without indignation. This is how he seems to expect the police to behave. Maurice, who has always viewed the police as his allies, is still feeling his own indignation, both at their superciliousness and their nonchalant brutality. When they pushed Sandford into the door, it was as if they were doing it for his benefit, knowing he was watching and had missed the rough stuff that had gone before. It is almost as if they recognised him as an outsider in this part of the city and were determined to demonstrate that he could not expect his usual deference down here.

Maurice suggests to Sandford that he might want to file a complaint against them.

Sandford looks shocked. 'No way.' He shakes his head. 'No way. They'd say it was an accident.'

'I'd be your witness,' says Maurice, wondering, even as he says the words, why he is so eager to be helpful. 'I saw exactly what they did. They shouldn't be allowed to get away with stuff like that.'

Again, Sandford shakes his head, wincing this time, perhaps from the movement of the pad against his wound. Maurice is even prepared, now he has a reason, to take him to hospital, just to emphasise the seriousness of the injury. By now, Sandford is rolling another cigarette. It seems to be a constant activity for him – he is either rolling or smoking one. He starts to light this while they are still in the kitchen. Once again, Maurice has to tell him not to smoke in his house.

'But it's not really your house, is it Maurice?' Sandford says.

'It belongs to me and my sisters. It has done for three years.'

Sandford says that as far as he is concerned this is Patricia's house.

'Well, you're wrong, and that's how the law would see it. It's my house and I live in it. Simple as that.'

'Why, Maurice? You've got that big place of your own.'

'How do you know about my place? How do you know how big it is?'

'Oh, I've seen it, Maurice,' he says. The cigarette still sits in the corner of his mouth, ready to be lit. It shudders in time with his words. 'I've been up there.'

'When?' says Maurice. He cannot be certain, but there seems to be something mildly threatening in Sandford's words.

Sandford ignores Maurice's question. 'Why do you need two houses?' he says.

Maurice has no inclination to explain to Sandford about his personal circumstances. The alternative – indeed, the obvious thing – would be to inform him, curtly but politely, that it isn't his business. But there is something in his attitude, something in his bearing that impels Maurice to speak. Perhaps it is a simple sense of reciprocity. After all, he has just been the beneficiary of an intimate revelation and he would quite like to hear some more. And sometimes, it's easier to speak than remain silent. He finds himself telling Sandford the story he wants to tell himself. It's a temporary separation, he tells him, a bit of time out for them both. The marriage has grown a little stale. It needs a kick-start, so he has decided to move out for a while. It's better to do it now, while he is between jobs. This way they won't get under one another's feet during the day.

Then he tells Sandford something he never intended to say, something that has not even occurred to him until the words pass his lips. He likes it here, he says. He was expecting to be lonely, bored. He was expecting to be a fish out of water, away from his house and his family, with no job, no one to see, nowhere to go during the day. He was expecting to feel acutely deprived here, dispossessed, bereaved even. But he doesn't.

Sandford hears him out in weary calm, watching him with his good eye, every now and then moving the unlit cigarette up to his mouth. Inattentively, he now lights it. Maurice does not try to stop him. Sandford inhales expansively and blows the smoke down to his feet. He takes several more drags while Maurice waits for him to speak, fussy little ones now, as though he is attempting to extract some unreachable essence. All he does, in response to Maurice, is nod every now and then. When he does open his mouth, it is to change the subject. He wants a lift back to his place.

'What's wrong with the bus?'

'I could wait an hour for a bus at this time of night,' he says. 'Then it might take another hour to get there. I can't handle that. It would be much quicker if you drove me.'

Put this way, it sounds a logical suggestion and at this moment Maurice does not feel averse to a drive. But it seems more important that he not accede to these demands. Sandford is already treating him with far more familiarity than Maurice would have believed possible if someone had described it to him beforehand and he feels it should be stopped. He considers claiming he's had too much to drink, a plausible excuse given that he's already eaten out that evening, but instead he says, 'I'm not moving the car at this time of night. I'd never get my parking spot back.'

He feels pleased to have given Sandford the weaker of the two excuses, as though by displaying his selfish motivations he has wrested back some control. It is telling, he thinks later, that he has felt the need to come up with an excuse at all. The same impetus prevented him from kicking Sandford out earlier, or from giving him up to the police. He suggests a taxi, but of course Sandford does not have the fare, in addition to which he complains again of a sore head. He speaks as though it is Maurice's responsibility to come up with the solution, even if that simply involves handing over money.

Tempting as it is to do so, just to get him out of the house, Maurice decides that the line has now been drawn. 'I'm not giving you money,' he says.

'Then what am I supposed to do?'

'It's not my problem.'

Suddenly Sandford yawns, violently and alarmingly. 'I could wait till morning,' he says. 'There'll be more buses in the morning, for sure.'

'You're not spending the night here.'

'Why not? There's plenty of room.'

Maurice looks at him, with his ridiculous black bandage, his half-closed eyes and his smelly little cigarette, and suddenly it seems a small price to pay to get him out of the house – in terms of the cost to his credibility for going back on his decision rather than the price in cash, of which he would happily pay many times the amount.

'All right,' he says, 'I'll pay the cab fare. I'll call you one now.'

Sandford thinks about this for a moment, then he says, 'OK, Maurice,' as though he is the one doing the favour. He yawns again. 'I want to sit down.'

Maurice motions him through to the other room while he makes the call, but Sandford is already walking, staggering under the archway and past the dining table towards the couch where, earlier that evening, Maurice enjoyed his anticipatory drink with his friend. Sandford leans on the furniture as he goes past, his knuckles white and taut against the backs of the dining chairs, against the table itself, against the wall, before groping his way around the couch and landing heavily on the cushions. Maurice watches him, then follows for a few steps. Even for Sandford, this sudden change is unsettling and Maurice has noticed he hasn't let go of his lighted cigarette, which is obviously going to need an ashtray. On the couch, he raises it to his lips, but his hand drops back down to his lap before he can position it to be smoked. His eyes are closed now. He lies against the back of the couch with his chin on his chest and his other arm raised and bent at the odd angle it assumed when he sat down. His feet are turned in towards each other and thin bubbles of saliva well between his lips. He appears to be unconscious.

*

The next couple of hours is a parade of visitors, of ever increasing urgency. First there is the cab driver, a tubby little fellow with a thick accent, who prises himself out of his seat to see for himself his passenger's condition and who insists Maurice call the emergency number. Next there is a paramedic, who arrives on a motorcycle equipped with a large box of tricks, a small selection of which are enough to convince him to call for an ambulance himself.

While they are waiting, Sandford appears to wake up. He blinks and rises to his feet muttering about the rabbit, sways one way then the other and collapses on the floor, in the process striking the other side of his head on the edge of the coffee table. While a trickle of brownish foam makes its way from the corner of his mouth to the carpet, the ambulance arrives, two men pushing a stretcher on its collapsible trolley through the narrow hallway. Sandford is wheeled out with the same utilitarian lack of ceremony with which the funeral hands wheeled Aunt Patricia to her final resting place. Maurice is invited to accompany them to the hospital, the choice appearing to be not so much whether he comes at all as whether he rides with them or makes his way by himself.

'Do you really need me there?' he asks.

'It would be useful,' says one of the ambulance men. 'They'll need someone to fill in forms, answer questions on his behalf.'

'I hardly know him,' Maurice says.

'Well, he's hardly capable of answering for himself.'

'Maybe you can do it.'

The ambulance man turns away, shaking his head.

As Maurice has not been in an ambulance before, he chooses to ride with them. He sits up at the front, and is treated to the rare spectacle of late night traffic parting before him whichever way they turn, along the short route to the hospital. Once there, he is able to confirm his ignorance of Sandford by failing to provide his address, his age, his next of kin, in fact anything about him except his name (even the first part of which he would not have known but for Mr Agarwal) and the manner by which he incurred his injury (falling down the stairs, he says, to a brief flicker of disbelief).

Under next of kin, they write his own name. 'We have to put someone,' they say.

# 7

The next morning, Maurice wakes late. He showers and dresses as normal. He comes downstairs, he makes tea. Sandford does not even cross his mind until he sees the couch on which he came to rest the night before. He feels a rising apprehension, a physical sensation inside his chest. It annoys him. Sandford has no business affecting him like this. He fills a bucket with hot water, dons rubber gloves and scrubs at the carpet where he left his spit, even though there is no stain and the thin dried crust is barely still visible. Maurice does not phone the hospital. He does not wish to promote his connection with Sandford, nor does he wish to feign interest in a ream of well-meaning progress reports. He goes for a walk, makes some phone calls.

Around noon, he receives a call from Sandford's landlord. Mr Agarwal launches into an elaborate explanation of who he is, but Maurice recognises him at once.

'I am calling you,' he announces, 'with reference to our pact.'

'Pact?' Maurice says, feeling a disproportionate unease at the implications of this word, which seems to have taken on a new meaning in the light of the previous night's events.

'A week has now passed,' he declares. 'It is time to report Patrick Sandford a missing person. Our pact, if you recall, was that one of us would do this.'

'It was, was it?' Maurice says, and explains, with some relief, that it is no longer necessary.

It comes as a relief to the other man as well. 'It must be a load off your mind that he has turned up safe and sound,' he says. 'I would not have mentioned it before while his whereabouts was causing you anxiety, but now that all is well would you be so kind as to inform him that he has fallen into arrears with his rent? If he wishes to keep the room, he will have to contact me by the end of this week.'

'I will let him know.'

'And tell me,' the landlord says, as they wind up their conversation, 'how is our friend's rabbit? Thriving, I hope?'

'Oh yes,' Maurice says, 'thriving.'

'I am pleased to hear it. However much one may dislike a creature, one doesn't like to think of it suffering.'

*

In the afternoon, the hospital calls Maurice with the news that scans have revealed no obvious damage and Sandford is ready to be discharged.

'I'm glad to hear it,' he says.

'When should I tell him to expect you?'

'Expect me?'

'To pick him up.'

'Isn't he capable of making his own way home?'

A brief silence ensues, after which there is a noticeable hardening in the tone of the woman's voice. 'Is there anybody else who could pick him up,' she says, 'if you're too busy?'

Maurice would have to sacrifice his parking spot to collect Sandford but not, as it happens, any pressing appointments. 'I can do it,' he says, 'but if he's ready to be discharged, then I'd have thought he should be capable of looking after himself.'

'Just because he doesn't need hospital care doesn't mean he doesn't need some looking after.'

'What sort of looking after?'

'He needs to be monitored. If his headache returns, we would want to see him again. And he must have complete rest. That means,' she says this with unmistakable relish, 'he'll need someone to do things for him.'

'It sounds like you want me to do your job for you.'

'We need the bed,' she says curtly. 'If you can't help out, I'll arrange for a home visit.'

'It's all right,' he says. 'I expect I'll manage.'

'And he'll need some clean clothes. When shall I tell him to expect you?'

In an unopened suitcase packed by his wife, Maurice finds various items of clothing he is not likely to wear again. He picks out for Sandford an old striped business shirt and the trousers from the suit in which he was married. It has been years since he has worn it, years in which his physique has shed all vestiges of its youthful trim. Instead of finding clothes to give away, he could, he supposes, simply lend them, and have them laundered afterwards, but somehow he feels these are things he will not want to wear again.

*

'You're the only person who hasn't asked me how I'm feeling today,' says Sandford, as Maurice escorts him back through his front door.

'That must make a change.'

'You have to look after me.'

'I know, I was told.'

Sandford lands heavily on the couch. The elaborate taping around his head has been replaced by a single large, neat, flesh-coloured sticking plaster and he is wearing Maurice's clothes, the trousers of which concertina around his ankles even when he is seated. The daylight accentuates his pasty complexion. Across his cheeks is a myriad of blemishes, tiny networks of broken veins, moles, pimples and rough shadowed regions where he might have neglected to shave. In addition, both his eyes are bloodshot and their pink rims look swollen and heavy.

He picks up the remote and aims it at the TV. A succession of images flickers across the screen, coming to rest on a program where a studio audience, all of whom seem to be female, black and overweight, whoop and applaud in chaotic unison.

'I'd rather you didn't watch TV,' Maurice says.

'Why?'

'Because I can't stand having that rubbish on all day.'

'You don't have to watch it.'

'I can't close my ears.'

'Why don't you go out?'

'This is my house!'

'What else am I supposed to do?'

Maurice has had almost identical conversations with his son, the only difference being that his son's is always a token protest undertaken in the knowledge that he will have to submit to Maurice's authority in the end. With Sandford, it is unclear how far this authority stretches. They are in his house, but as far as Sandford is concerned even that is a matter for dispute. Sandford is also his patient, in a way, which surely gives him some authority for a different reason. But if Sandford chooses to defy him, it is hard to see what he can do about it.

Sandford mutters something, which he doesn't catch. Maurice asks him to repeat it.

Sandford clears his throat with a long low gargle. 'The pompous one,' he says. 'That's what Patricia used to call you.'

Maurice says nothing. He is taken aback, but at first it is more by the fact of Patricia talking about him at all than by what she is supposed to have said. His first thought is to question her right to even hold an opinion on him, let alone one as sardonic as this, let alone to share it with anyone. He would never have imagined her indulging in gossip. He would never have imagined her even having opinions of her own. As with the revelation about the coffee, it lays bare a dimension of her life whose existence has never occurred to him. He finds himself quite surprised by the extent to which this shocks him.

Sandford spends the rest of the afternoon lying across the couch, smoking and watching TV. With both activities he has somehow managed to defy Maurice, to manoeuvre him into a position from which Maurice realises he does not really care. It reminds Maurice of the dog they had soon after they were married, which he had been determined would live outside – either the dog was not trainable or its determination was greater than Maurice's, for within a few months he had given up and it was sleeping on one of the couches.

In the evening, Maurice opens a can of soup but Sandford isn't hungry. Unable to reclaim his space without talking to him, Maurice goes to bed early, leaving him there on the couch, still dozing with the remote in his hand.

*

The next morning, Sandford is up first. Maurice hears him in the bathroom, taking a long shower.

'You look better,' he says, when he sees him downstairs.

Sandford is smoking, of course, but outside the front of the house this time. He nods. He has washed his hair. It looks light and wiry where before it had been plastered down against his scalp – more like steel wool now than lead.

'I feel better,' he says. 'Yesterday I didn't feel good.'

'If you're better, you can go back home.'

Sandford looks puzzled.

'To the place where you live,' Maurice says. 'You can't stay here forever.'

'They said it'd be a couple of days at least, Maurice. I can't go yet.'

'You don't have to take too much notice of what they say. They're just covering themselves.'

But Sandford slowly shakes his head. In that gesture, there is a glimpse of the day before, an aversion to sudden movement in case something comes loose. Maurice has been misled by his general air of cleanness. He resigns himself to another day with him.

'I need some clothes,' Sandford says, as if to confirm Maurice's thinking. He is still wearing Maurice's, which are creased and wrinkled as though he has slept in them, which he probably has.

'I'll tell you what,' Maurice says, 'after breakfast I'll drive you over there. You can pick up some of your own clothes and bring them back.'

But he does not want to do that either. His place is too far away. His idea is to go down to the charity shop and pick out what he needs from there. That is what he used to do, he says, before Patricia gave him the use of her washing machine. It was cheaper than getting the old ones cleaned.

'OK, fine,' Maurice shrugs.

'I'll need some money,' he says.

'You're expecting me to give you money as well?'

'As well as what?'

'As well as everything else. As well as driving you around, as well as having you as a guest in my home.' Even as he says these words, Maurice is aware that his actions are nowhere near as generous as his words would have them be. It has been no real trouble. In spite of everything, he has actually quite liked having someone else in the house, even if that someone is Sandford.

'How can I buy them without money? What do you expect me to do, Maurice?'

'I don't understand how you can have no money. What would you have done if you hadn't had me to ask?'

'I had my things here.' He motions with his head to the room directly above them. 'That was my money, Maurice.'

Rather than just give him cash, Maurice decides to accompany him to the shop. He doesn't have anything pressing to do just now and the idea appeals of doing something, anything different. They share the ten-minute walk in silence. This is something Maurice notices about Sandford – he rarely speaks unless he has something to say, more often than not a question to which he wants to know the answer, otherwise he seems quite comfortable with silence. It has not occurred to him before how unusual this is. He tries to resist the impulse to chat, to make conversation as they walk. It is something he imagines Sandford would despise.

This must be the shop where his sisters deposited the rest of Sandford's things. He feels mildly anxious in case he recognises some of it there, not because he feels any particular sense of guilt or responsibility – after all, they cleaned it out in good faith – but more because it might require him to elaborate on the lie he has already started. Sandford strikes him as someone who would have little difficulty seeing through untruths, either because he is adept at lying himself or because he is constitutionally incapable of telling one – Maurice has not yet worked out which is the more likely. He could come clean, of course, and simply recompense him for all these things of his, but that would feel too much like a backward step.

It is Maurice's first time inside a charity shop. An aroma of baked-on sweat lingers in every corner, but it is densely stocked and the clothes are prismatically grouped on their racks, which gives the place a surprising air of efficiency. Sitting on a chair by the window, a woman with long grey hair is loudly carrying on what he initially takes to be a dialogue with the woman at the desk but which, by the time they exit the shop a few minutes later, has revealed itself to be domineeringly one-sided. Evidently this is a hazard of working in places like this, to have street people come in and make themselves at home.

Sandford is not a discerning shopper. He quickly locates the racks that hold the clothes he is after and he selects a handful of T-shirts, a denim jacket and a pair of suit trousers which, in spite of Maurice's urging, he does not try on.

In one of the aisles, two women are holding up dresses against themselves with the sort of freedom that would be stifled by sales staff in a normal shop. Maurice even casts his own appraising eye over the kitchen utensils and china to see if there is anything he could possibly imagine buying, but Sandford is keen to leave. In his world, there is no room for browsing. He wants a coffee, he says.

'I've got some in the kitchen,' says Maurice, but Sandford wants to go out. He wants to go to a café.

Even though Maurice has nothing to do for the rest of the morning, his first thought is to invent an errand for himself. He rarely goes to cafés. He always despised the culture that seemed to have taken root in his office; 'we're going for coffee' each morning had somehow become an accepted part of the working day. To him, it was just an excuse to loaf for half an hour. If Maurice wanted a coffee, he had someone bring it to his desk. However, he is not at the office now and there is nothing to loaf from. He would never have imagined himself thinking this, but a visit to a café will give him something to do.

The place Sandford wants to go is a little way down the main street. They enter through a bookshop, and squeeze down a passageway to the counter, where they place their orders. Sandford asks for coffee in some style or other, then lingers over the little cake display before making his selection. His new trousers are not as long as Maurice's, but they are still too large for him. He had been prepared to walk the street holding them up with one hand until Maurice lent him a belt.

Maurice repeats Sandford's order for himself.

'You get good coffee here,' Sandford assures him, in a rare display of ingratiation.

Maurice peels a couple of notes from his wallet and pays. Sandford makes no acknowledgement of this gesture. Maurice is only doing what seems to be expected. They wend their way through another doorway and emerge into a paved courtyard, where they find themselves a table under the shade of a banana palm. At the next table, a girl, presumably a student, types frowningly at her computer. Nearby, a young man, wearing a beanie despite the day's warmth, sits by himself smoking home-rolled, tobacco pouch open on the table in front of him as though it is the source of all benedictions. Farther away, at a table next to the brightly decorated toilet wall, a pair of sapphicly undecorated women sit in companionable silence while a large basset hound snoozes at their feet. It is quiet and sun-dappled, as though they have stepped into another, enchanted, reality.

Sandford watches as Maurice puts his money back into his wallet, stuffing the notes in amongst the others that are stacked together like a closed-up fan.

'You like money, don't you, Maurice?'

Maurice is unsure how to respond. 'Don't we all?' he says.

'I expect you make a good amount.'

'I did all right.'

'What was your job?'

'It's hard to explain,' says Maurice. But because they have the rest of the morning, and probably the afternoon as well, he decides to give Sandford a brief overview of the industry as a whole culminating, if he is still interested, with an explanation of his part in it.

Sandford listens while he describes some of the different ways they make money out of money at the big end of town. As he pauses to drink his coffee after giving a slightly more complex account than he intended of the concept of brokerage, Sandford interrupts him.

'What do you actually make, Maurice?' he says.

'I make money,' says Maurice, without thinking.

'I don't mean like that.'

'What do you mean?'

'Like this table, for instance.' He slaps his hand down. 'Someone's made this table and sold it for a living. It's useful.'

'Do you think what I do isn't useful?'

'I don't think anything. I don't understand it. I'm just asking.'

'Well, OK, I'll tell you why what we do is useful.' And Maurice gives the little speech he has given a dozen times before, whenever the worth of what he does is questioned; how the industry is vital for the health of the economy for the simple reason that they maximise the efficiency of every dollar that's in circulation. 'We make money work,' he says. 'We keep it fit.'

'Like giving it a workout?' Sandford says.

'Yes, if you like.'

'It can't be working that hard if there's so much left for you people to cream off the top.'

'It wouldn't have been there in the first place if it wasn't for us.'

'Yes, it would. It just belonged to someone else.'

Sandford makes this statement with such direct simplicity that Maurice is momentarily thrown. He does not know how to respond.

'Why is it better that it goes to you?'

'I don't think that's the point,' is all Maurice can think to say.

'I do. I think the people who produce the tables should get the money. They are doing something useful.'

They both look down at the table between them. It's a pleasing square shape, its surface is made of some sort of polished metal folded down under each side like the wrapping on a present. The surface is blemish free but in the light it shows thousands of tiny scratches that seem to change direction depending on the viewing angle. It is solid and dependable, perfect in its design.

They finish the rest of their coffee in silence. The palm leaf over Maurice's head moves slightly, changing the position of the little patches of sunlight, rearranging them across his back. He doesn't want to be talking about his job or the economy, or money, or tables.

He is still thinking about Patricia's description of him. 'The pompous one'. It is a word Maurice would never have imagined being in her vocabulary. It seems to further highlight the fact that he has never thought of her as a fully functioning adult, with views and opinions and her own way of expressing them. Maurice only ever treated her as he would a child, to be tolerated, indulged perhaps, but never considered as equal. 'Pompous'. The word opens up a whole new realm of possibilities. It speaks of a certain insight, a discernment he had never seen in her. Used in conversation with Sandford, it indicates a mind not without its own brand of subversive irony, a woman quite capable of independent thought and gently pricking the bubble of those who misread her. Her relationship with Sandford, which Maurice has never actually contemplated beyond the general awareness he has gleaned, suddenly blossoms in front of him. He sees that they must have held conversations, related to each other the stories of their lives, spent hours at a time in one another's company.

'Is this where you and Patricia used to meet?' he says.

Sandford nods and stirs his coffee. He has added three sachets of sugar from the bowl on the table.

'How did you first meet her?'

('The pompous one'. Does that mean Patricia had nicknames for the others as well, his sisters and his cousin? Or was it just him?)

'I first met her here,' Sandford says. 'I was sitting over there,' he points to a table against the wall where a ponytailed man of Maurice's age is unfolding his newspaper at the crossword page, 'and she was sitting here, where you are. She called over to me. She wanted to know where she could get some heroin.'

'The drug?'

'Yes.'

'Did she know what she was asking?'

'Oh yes, Maurice.'

'And were you able to help her?'

'Not with the heroin, no.'

'What on earth did she want heroin for?'

'Boredom and loneliness,' Sandford says, with his brutal simplicity.

It turns out that Patricia knew as much about illegal drugs as Maurice would have expected her to. She got the idea from a TV documentary in which a young addict was asked how she first came to use it. 'Boredom and loneliness' had been her reply. The interviewer then asked her whether heroin had helped, expecting some conventional expression of regret for the waste of her youth, but the woman replied that it had. It had helped.

'So what did you do?'

'I became her friend, Maurice.' He lights his cigarette, blows out a long wisp of smoke. 'She didn't even have anyone to change a light bulb for her.'

In a sudden access of the obvious, it occurs to Maurice that instead of simply picking Patricia up and dropping her off on those occasional Sundays, he could have spent a few minutes in her house, changing light bulbs, moving furniture, taking the lids off jam jars. Not only could, but should. It had never occurred to him at the time, so convinced had he been of the merit of what he was doing for her, that there could be anything more she might need. If he had thought about it at all, he would, he supposes, have assumed that she had someone she could call on, a neighbour perhaps, and of course she had – Sandford. But he never asked.

Maurice is not a man who normally feels shame but he does now, a little, at his former self.

**8**

He hears nothing of Sandford until the following week, when he receives a phone call from someone who identifies himself as the manager of a pub, the Wheatsheaf Hotel or something, up near where Sandford has his room. He has applied for a job there, it appears, and he has named Maurice as his referee.

'Why did he leave you?' is the first question Maurice is asked.

He thinks quickly. The literal truth is not required here. The question is, how can he bend it and still remain a) plausible and b) within the bounds of the rules that apply to these things? Evidently Sandford is relying on him and honesty will serve no purpose. How can Maurice say he does not deserve a chance? He only wishes Sandford had given him some warning, then they might have been able to come up with a consistent story.

'He just wanted to move on,' he says vaguely. 'But while he was with me, I only ever found him to be competent and honest. What type of job are you considering him for?'

The man mentions something about bar work, cleaning, handing out the winnings from the poker machines.

'He'll be fine at that,' Maurice tells him, recalling the two occasions when Sandford rose from the couch to help out in the kitchen, once to wash up after using the last of the coffee mugs and another time to sweep the floor after breaking one. 'In all the time he was here, I've never known anyone so willing to help out wherever it was needed.' For this claim, Maurice is able to use as his yardstick his own son, who has never, to his knowledge, volunteered for a domestic task.

'And how long did he work for you?'

By this time, Maurice has assessed the man as easy to dominate. His voice is thin and he hesitates in reaction to Maurice's replies. This might be the first time he has ever phoned anyone for a reference.

Maurice feigns an interruption. 'Excuse me,' he says, and holds the phone to his chest while he clatters things about on the table. He lets this go on for the best part of a minute, guessing that the man is the sort of person who would be loath to impose on the time of someone so obviously busy.

'I'm sorry about that,' he says at last, 'where were we? Oh yes, Patrick Sandford. No, I never had any trouble with him at all. One of the best people I've had here. I'd have him back tomorrow if I could.'

'Thank you,' he says, 'thank you for your time.'

'Not at all,' says Maurice, feeling better than he has for days at this rare chance to exercise his prestige.

*

That same day, Maurice is visited for the first time by his son and his wife. They drive across in the late afternoon to collect the bicycle he has been keeping for the boy. It has been propped against the wall outside the back door, unknown, as far as Maurice is aware, to Sandford, its rightful owner. He would have seen it if he had ever taken out the rubbish or entered the laundry, but he had rarely left the couch.

Maurice's wife walks in with the barely suppressed agitation of someone who has made themselves a promise to behave in a way that goes against their nature. In her case, it is to repress the urge to comment on Maurice's living arrangements. The dining room, for instance, is a mess of coffee mugs, toast-crumbed plates, books, magazines and other bits and pieces that have accumulated for want of an appointed resting place. In her own home, she would have a mess like this shipshape in five minutes flat – mugs and plates straight into the dishwasher, books returned to their shelves (and carefully bookmarked if they have been left open), magazines neatly stacked and relegated back to the coffee table, other paraphernalia swept into a box and placed out of sight on a prearranged shelf in a cupboard.

Maurice appreciates the restraint with which she now surveys this scene while he retires to the kitchen to boil the kettle. He has to admit that it contains an element of provocation, as he has deliberately left his breakfast things out after the boy's call to tell him they are coming – and on finishing her tea she takes the opportunity to include as many as possible of them in her visit to the kitchen to return her own mug.

She does not want to appear to be making herself at home on what is his territory, so when she finally seats herself it is to perch awkwardly on the edge of one of the wooden chairs. She is dressed in what might be termed formal attire, a soft red woollen skirt and jacket, with a brooch and perfume to match. She looks as if she is going to visit…a great-aunt. Maurice hears the crackle of her stocking as she crosses her legs and gives the skirt's hem a prim little tug down towards her knee. He has never liked stockings or tights. To him, nylon is a hostile fabric, unkind to the touch. In their early days together, it was a private joke of theirs that she would never wear them, for ease of access. Now it looks as though she has dressed up specially to come here. The sheer presence of these barriers brings to mind what they conceal, the flesh of which he knows every inch.

'You seem to have settled in,' she says.

Maurice nods. Over on the couch near the television, Sandford's pillows and blankets remain as he last had them. Maurice has not used the TV since his departure and so has not had occasion to set foot in that part of the room.

His wife cannot help herself. 'You've had someone staying?'

It occurs to Maurice later that the evidence showing his guest so obviously not sharing his bed must have emboldened her.

'It was someone who knew Aunt Patricia,' he says. 'Someone from the funeral.'

'Not that weird guy with the rabbit?' the boy pipes up, emerging from his own private tour of the upstairs. This is the first time he has been here since Maurice moved in.

'Yes,' he says, 'the very same.'

'The rabbit you left with us?' says his wife.

'That's right.'

Maurice gives her a brief version of the whole story so he can make clear  that the events that had led to Sandford staying here had not been his responsibility.

'By the way,' he calls to his son, who has made his way over to the couch and is now exercising the remote. 'I hope you haven't got too attached to it.'

His son looks over the back of the couch at him. 'Why?' he says warily.

At the same time, Maurice's wife recrosses her legs. (Crackle crackle, goes the nylon.)

'Because he wants it back. I forgot to tell you before.'

The boy directs his stare from one parent to the other, then he turns back to the television. The ball is in her court, it seems.

'There's a problem there,' she says. 'I'm afraid it's disappeared.'

'Disappeared? What do you mean?'

'We let it out on the grass and it ran away.'

'Mum was supposed to be watching it,' says the boy helpfully.

'I thought it would be all right,' she says. 'How was I supposed to know the stupid thing would make a dash for it straight into the plumbago? I thought they liked the grass.'

'But surely it was still inside the fence?' Maurice says.

'There are holes in the fence,' she says. 'Everywhere.'

This last word is a direct reproach to Maurice, her opportunity to divert attention from her own negligence to his. Although it has been long established that they pay someone else to do these kinds of repairs, all aspects of yard maintenance are still somehow Maurice's responsibility.

He says, 'If I'd known you were going to let a pet rabbit loose on the lawn, I'd have had the fence checked immediately.'

'No, you wouldn't,' she says. 'You never do.'

She is sitting back in her chair, Maurice notices, visibly more relaxed now she is able to resume a familiar role. He says nothing, not because she is right, which she is, but because the prospect of a quarrel bores him. In spite of the upheaval of the past few weeks, the trauma of being exiled from his old environment and having to adapt to this new one, he feels much more at ease without her continual scrutiny.

To help his mother along, the boy pipes up again from the couch, this time without shifting his eyes from the TV. 'She never even watched it,' he says. 'She just went straight back inside.'

'I was putting out the washing. If you'd lift a finger to help once in a while…'

'You told me you'd watch it,' he repeats, with his child's merciless focus.

'And what were you doing?' Maurice asks him.

'I don't know,' he says. 'If she'd asked me to watch it, I would have, but she said she was going to.'

It seems fair enough. Maurice sits back, satisfied with his token show of support.

'I've got enough going on as it is,' his wife says, turning to him. 'Why should I be expected to look after rabbits too?'

'If you'd asked me…'

But she has found her path and she does not wish to be diverted from it. Maurice sits there while she spins the familiar line about her busy life, the juggling act of maintaining a household, bringing up a teenage boy, living on her own – at one point she even uses the term 'single mother'. Even though Maurice is determined not to take part in the row she is brewing, she presses on, acting out his side in addition to her own. Yes, she says, she has brought it on herself, she knows that and there is no need to have it pointed out, but what he has to remember is that he had hardly been there anyway and she has done little more than formalise an arrangement that had already been in existence for some years. And he need not start on about how he has been busy earning a living for them. Whatever he might claim, the fact is he has organised things so that he is hardly ever home, and if he does not accept that, one only has to look at him when he was there, his irritability, his general inattentiveness. It would not surprise her if he was finding the new circumstances to his liking.

And so it goes on, the litany of reproach and accusation, none unjustified but all delivered with such relentless allusion to what he is now being spared that his concentration starts to flag. He finds himself fantasising once more, imagining her thighs naked, stockingless, the pale and slightly puffy flesh up near her behind, the occasional hair she might have missed that only he, with his intimate access, would ever know about, the response he was able to elicit, in spite of her icy facade, by working those secret spots. And all the while her voice, lowered out of their son's hearing, gathers intensity to match each further layer of accusation, pinning Maurice to his seat with its own version of all this remembered intimacy.

He has to stop her mid-sentence, pretend he has something to check in the kitchen, in case he finds himself down on his knees, begging her to take him back.

He stays out there for a few minutes, recovering his poise. She does not follow him, as she would once have done. While he is there, he makes more tea, consciously rattling cups and saucers to establish the legitimacy of his actions. He knows he does not have to justify them now, in his own house, but he is still acting out of deference to her.

When he comes back in, she is still sitting in the same position. He gives her more tea, even though she has not asked for it, which she accepts as though she has.

The boy has found the cartoon channel, and the crude, washed-out shapes flicker across the screen in the corner.

'When are you going to come and stay with me here?' Maurice calls over to him.

'I don't know,' he says, without turning round. Then, as if responding to the prompt his mother has wilfully suppressed, he sits up and faces her over the back of the couch. 'It's no good for school,' he mumbles.

'What do you mean?'

'It's too far to go to school from here.'

'He walks to school from home,' Maurice's wife says. 'If he stayed with you, he'd have to bus and train it, unless you were willing to drive him. I thought you might have found somewhere a bit closer.'

'This isn't costing us anything,' Maurice reminds her.

She says nothing. He leaves the implied reproach hanging for a moment.

'Maybe you can come over at the weekend,' Maurice says.

'Maybe.' He slides back down onto the couch.

'Why don't you come up to see him?' his wife says.

'I will when rugby starts. I'll be up there two or three times a week.'

She puts down her cup. 'Hasn't he told you?'

'Told me what?'

'He's not playing this year.' She straightens her skirt and gives another prim little nod, as though Maurice is receiving his just deserts for his neglect.

In a flash, he sees the collapse of the social life he'd had mapped out for himself over the winter. If his son isn't playing, he won't be able to coach. If he doesn't coach, he will have no position at the club, and the weekly pub meetings with the other rugby fathers will carry on without him. He had been counting on it to help fill the void. He'd been looking forward to it more than he had realised.

'Is this true?' he calls over.

'What?' The boy does not look up this time.

'That you're giving up rugby?'

'Um…'

'Of course it's true,' his wife says. 'The only reason he played for so long was because of you. He's old enough now to make up his own mind. He wants to play soccer instead.' She tries to conceal it, but the little note of triumph is too strong. It is there, in the extra second with which she holds Maurice's stare, and the beginnings of another prim little nod.

'So that's the end of coaching for me.'

'Coach his soccer team.'

'I don't know anything about soccer.'

'For Christ's sake, Maurice, it's not about you.'

She never wanted their son to play rugby. Like most mothers, she frets over the risk of injury. Now it seems she has got her way. Maurice might claim it has happened the moment his back is turned, but he knows what she says is true, that his son has only ever played to please him. As a youngster, he was bigger than his teammates and, urged on by his father's enthusiasm, he had been a lynchpin of his teams. But over the last couple of years, the other kids have caught up with him and he has lumbered around the paddock with no natural skills to make up for his lost physical prestige. This new development is a blow to Maurice alone.

With this little triumph behind her, his wife relaxes further. For the first time since sitting down, she looks around her, taking in the room's cavernous decrepitude. 'It's a big place for one person,' she says. 'It makes you wonder what she did with herself all day.'

Quite apart from the fact that she is living in a house three times the size of this one, Maurice now finds himself taking exception to her not referring to his aunt by name. 'You mean Patricia,' he says.

'Yes, poor Aunt Patricia. What on earth did she do here? She can't have spent her whole time making those stupid collages.'

'What?' Based on what he has discovered so far, he had been about to offer some insights. Was he the only person not to know about them?

'Those pictures she used to collect. She always had some in her bag. She used to ask me my opinion sometimes.'

'Yes, yes,' says Maurice dismissively. 'I know what you're talking about. We found them in her wardrobe. They were quite elaborate things actually.'

His wife shrugs and swallows the rest of her tea.

'What else did she talk to you about?'

'Oh, I don't know, Maurice. This and that.'

Did she ever say anything about me, he wants to ask, did she tell her that he was pompous as well?

'I found them quite moving actually, the collages,' he says.

His wife says nothing. She is not used to hearing him talk like this.

'Yes,' he continues. 'The idea of her alone in this house, day after day, waking up every morning with the whole day stretching out in front of her, wondering how she was going to fill it. It wouldn't have been easy.'

She is uncomfortable. She pulls the hem of her skirt down over her knees again. 'What are you going on about?' she says.

'Those faces were a way of surrounding herself with people. She didn't have any in real life, you see, so she collected them from magazines.'

'Yes, yes, Maurice, I understand what you're saying.'

'In fact, I'd say she was something of an artist.'

'Artist! What would you know about that?' she scoffs, in the hope that he is joking. He isn't.

'You didn't much care for her, did you?'

'I don't know what you're trying to do here, Maurice, but...' She stops. She will not be drawn. She closes her eyes and takes a quiet breath in the way she has that is supposed to demonstrate her desire for calm. It also serves as a way of cutting off any further discussion of the subject.

He closes his own eyes for a second, and imagines he is alone in the room.

'I'm sorry about the rabbit,' she now says. 'I'll replace it, I promise. I'll go to the pet shop tomorrow.'

'Don't worry about it,' he says, content himself to have the subject changed. 'It can't have been that important to him, otherwise he wouldn't have asked a complete stranger to look after it in the first place.'

'But it was my fault.'

'Honestly, it's all right. I'll handle it.'

'I feel bad about it,' she says, 'I really think I should do something.'

Maurice tells her to go ahead and do as she pleases. He wants her out of the house. It is exhausting him to have every conversational turn find its way down this familiar track. He wants to live in a different world, where history does not hang so heavy, where words are not burdened by such weight of meaning, where people ask questions because they want to understand things, not because they want their agendas confirmed. For a mad second or two, he even wishes Sandford was here.

**9**

Boredom and loneliness; every day, it seems, Maurice gains another insight into the kind of life Patricia lived. For the first time in his own life, he is faced with a daily struggle to find something to do with himself. This is quite new to him. For the past two decades, every spare minute has been given over to work in some form or other. Time to himself has been rare, luxurious and fiercely guarded. At least, this is what he has told himself and it is easy to do so when it never amounts to more than the odd few minutes snatched from a busy schedule. Now it's all different. It's the other way round. It's back to front and turned on its head. He has never had as much time as he has now and he has never had so little use for it.

He begins to understand the elaborate routines his wife has built up for herself. He wonders how Patricia coped, whether she used to do something the same. At least he has things to look forward to – finding a new job, seeing his son. Patricia would have had nothing – just Sandford, latterly, and photos cut out of magazines.

Without the familiar frameworks, there is very little around which to construct his days. It is as though he has to reinvent himself every morning. He's lucky, says an ex-colleague when he talks to him on the phone. What wouldn't he give for a break, a bit of time out of the hurly-burly. He should enjoy it while he can. But Maurice has always disdained idleness.

He begins to spend a disproportionate amount of time on the many small tasks that are needed to maintain a household – cleaning and shopping and the like. He washes the dishes and wipes the bench tops after every meal. He empties the rubbish daily and he embarks on a gradual but satisfying quest to remove all the mould from the bathroom tiles. He spends a lot of time just walking, and begins to think nothing of strolling down to the shops several times a day to pick up groceries as he thinks of them. He never writes lists, in the unacknowledged hope that his forgetfulness will give him an excuse to go out again. He becomes adept at seeking out bargains, not because he needs to save money (although he does, it turns out) as for the simple exercise of it. Maurice has not been the sort to shop around. If he wants to buy something, he goes out and does so without a thought for the cost. Bargain-hunting has always reeked, to him, of failure. Now suddenly he is content to spend a whole morning searching for the perfect, cut-price dish rack.

He starts a new morning routine of walking down to the café with the newspaper, where he sits with his coffee and cake and does the crossword. He learns the names of one or two of the staff, and they learn his. The women with the basset hound are there most days and it is not long before he starts to exchange greetings with them as well. He begins to feel as though he is part of an exclusive, hidden community. Timed judiciously, he can make this activity last for most of the morning, which only gives him the afternoons to fill. Sometimes this takes him back to the café, where he repeats his routine from the morning, with a different newspaper. Occasionally, and with a frequency that diminishes in almost direct proportion to the passage of time, there will be an interview for a job, or a meeting to sound out the possibility of a position, or even a lunch with one of the few ex-colleagues who is still prepared to talk to him, during which his options are canvassed. Invariably, and with sinking inevitability, these come to nothing.

After a while, it starts to take an effort of will to stir himself at all. Even when he does make plans, it is a struggle to see them through. He begins to appreciate the reality that underpins some people's lives – that it is easier to do nothing. The only distractions he can rouse himself to pursue are temporary and trivial ones – coffee, walking, crossword puzzles. Without the familiar structures, he has nothing to fall back on.

So it is with a certain frisson of irresponsibility that, a couple of weeks after he saw him last, he takes in Sandford's voice on the other end of the phone.

That last time, he had been bundling up his clothes into a shopping bag and walking out of the door and, Maurice assumed at the time, out of his life. As it closed behind him, Maurice had convinced himself of the idea of a burden removed. Now he would be loath to portray himself as glad to hear the familiar voice, but he does find himself responding with a surprising degree of goodwill.

'Maurice,' he says, 'I need your help.'

'What is it?' says Maurice. 'Why do you need my help?'

'Can you help me or not?'

There is an edge to his voice. It could be desperation, hysteria even. It is something Maurice has not heard in Sandford before. In the absence of any further information, this is the choice Sandford is giving him; to brand himself as a person who helps, or not. The correct answer has to be no.

'Yes, I can help you,' he says.

Within the hour, Sandford is knocking on his door. He is wearing what appears to be the same suit he wore to Patricia's funeral and his hair is combed straight across his forehead in a way that proclaims art-lessness and innocence. Before coming in, he wipes his feet, even though the weather is dry and his shoes are not dirty.

'I lost my job,' he says.

'That's no good,' says Maurice, warily now. 'You'll have to find another one.'

'It's not as easy as that.' He gulps with the nervous tic that seems to take over his face whenever he isn't smoking.

Maurice ushers him into the dining room, where he takes a seat at the table. A scar is visible on his forehead behind a gap in his fringe. It is pink and livid, as though he has recently picked off the scab.

He pats his coat pockets, locates his tobacco pouch and places it on the table. Then he seems to remember something. 'Do you mind if I smoke?' he says.

'No,' Maurice waves him on, approving of this new deferential tone. 'Go ahead.'

Sandford goes through the familiar routine, spreading the tobacco along the crease of the paper, rolling it into a tube and touching it to the tip of his tongue, the whole operation taking only a few seconds. Maurice watches with fascination, no less than the first time he saw it. In some way he doesn't understand, he envies Sandford this simple routine. Even the act of watching it makes him feel refreshed, fully attentive for a few seconds.

Sandford calms down once he has the cigarette alight and has sucked in a few mouthfuls of smoke. 'The thing is,' he says, 'I haven't just been sacked. They want to press charges.'

'For what?'

'They're saying I stole money off them.'

'Why would they say that?'

'They had me doing the cashing up,' he says. 'I had to take the money from the till into a little room at the back. Then I had to sort it, count it and put it in the safe. There was nobody else there. I'd never handled that much money before…' Sandford is sitting forward on the seat, gesturing with his hands in a way he has not done before. With splayed fingers, he traces the size and wonder of what he had been faced with in that little room.

'So what did you do?'

'I took it away with me.'

'You took it home?'

He seems startled. 'Yes.'

'How much?'

'Three thousand, two hundred and forty dollars.'

'You stole over three thousand dollars from them? What made you think you could get away with it?'

'I didn't. I mean, I didn't think about that.'

'What did you think about?'

'I don't know. Nothing much. I just liked having the money. I liked being able to hold it and look at it. Why shouldn't I?'

'What were you intending to do with it?'

'I don't know.' Sandford shrugs, as if to emphasise his helplessness throughout. He looks down into the stub of his cigarette, a short used empty tube tipped by a glowing red bead. He pushes the bead out with his thumb and watches it smoulder on a breakfast plate. The smoke ceases within seconds. 'I was going to give it back.'

Maurice laughs, and is somehow surprised when Sandford does not do the same. It is hardly worth addressing this last remark. He decides to ignore it.

'Sounds like you're in trouble,' he says. 'What do you think I can do about it?'

'I thought,' Sandford says, 'you might be able to intervene on my behalf.'

'With who?'

'The hotel. The police.'

'You have a very mistaken idea of my influence if you think that would do you any good.'

'There's nobody else I could ask. You're the only person I know they might listen to.'

'There must be somebody else,' says Maurice. He senses an opportunity to find out more about Sandford's background. 'Don't you have family somewhere?'

Sandford sniffs and gives a little roll of his eyes.

'Well, don't you?'

'I had Patricia.'

'She wasn't family, though.'

'She was, to me.'

'Did she ever have to do this sort of thing for you?'

'No.' He does not sound affronted at the suggestion that this might have happened before. 'They'd never have listened to her. They'd listen to you, though.'

Maurice likes what he hears. Yes, he thinks, that's me. People do listen to me. Even now.

'What exactly are you expecting me to say?'

'That it was out of character or something, you know.'

'How do I know it was out of character?'

'How do you know it wasn't?'

'Exactly. I don't know anything about you.'

'What do you want to know?'

'I want to know enough that I can be sure of what I'm telling some-one about you. You can cut out all the bullshit for a start.'

'What do you mean, Maurice? What bullshit?'

'The bullshit about how you were going to give it back, how you just wanted to look at it. You stole it, plain and simple, and you got caught. And don't tell me it's the first time you've stolen something.'

Sandford nods his head to one side and then the other, as though assessing the balance of merit on either side. Then he nods in the middle. 'All right, Maurice, I admit I stole it. But what I said was true. I did want to be able to hold the money. I'd never seen that much before. And I didn't have any plans for it. Taking it back was an option.'

'Oh, for goodness sake!'

'I'm not lying, Maurice. I'm not a liar.'

Maurice continues to express his disbelief.

'What about you? Why don't you come clean about a few things?'

'Such as what?'

'My bike.'

'What bike?'

'You know what bike. You had it outside the back door. You thought I didn't see it there, but I did.'

'I didn't know it was yours.'

'How did you not know? It was in the room up there, with all my other things. There were two of them.'

'I didn't know it was yours,' Maurice insists. 'I assumed it belonged to my aunt. It was her house. I gave it to my son. I'll get it back for you.'

Sandford seems pacified, but only for a moment. 'What about every-thing else?'

Maurice wonders whether it is safe to continue denying all knowledge of it. But there isn't time to follow the various arguments to their conclusion. He decides not to try. Perhaps Sandford has forgotten about his previous denials.

'I'm afraid I can't do much about that now. It's gone. Maybe I can give you money for it. Anyway, this is all irrelevant. You said you wanted help. Why don't we work out what I can do to help you?'

'It's not irrelevant, Maurice. It shows you'd steal too, given the opportunity.'

'I didn't steal your things. We thought it belonged to Patricia, and therefore we had the right to dispose of it in any way we saw fit.'

'But you didn't say that before. You denied all knowledge of it. You let me think someone else had stolen it.'

The bonds of Maurice's untruths begin to slip. Perhaps it was stealing, what he did. 'Look,' he says. 'I've offered to reimburse you for everything.'

'You're just like me, Maurice.'

'I'm nothing like you.'

'You're right, I think you're worse.'

'What do you mean?'

'I intended to pay that money back in the first place. You're only offering now, after you've been caught out.'

Sandford takes out his tobacco pouch and rolls another cigarette. The process is completed within seconds. Once again, Maurice watches the familiar finger movements, the almost implausible dexterity of those stubby digits. Sandford places the unlit cigarette on the table. A stray tobacco strand hangs from one end. He is sitting forward now, his elbows on his knees, head perched between his shoulders. His head resembles an egg that is too large for its nest.

Maurice is not normally at a loss for words, but he cannot think of anything to say. The only thing that seems worth saying is to agree that the two of them are alike, that he deserves everything that is going to happen to him. His empty breakfast mug is on the round wooden corner of the table. It has a blue and white enamel design, one of a series his wife packed for him. She had not liked using them because the rims were too thick. Sandford traces his finger over the blue lines of the pattern.

'Yes,' says Maurice, 'a cup of tea. Why don't I make us a cup of tea?'

Sandford nods.

'And then you can tell me exactly what it is you're expecting me to do for you.'

He goes into the kitchen. The soles of his shoes squeak loudly as he crosses from carpet to lino. He fills the kettle, pushing the open spout right up into the tap while he runs the water, then returns it, satisfyingly heavy, to its cradle. He flicks the switch. But he has flicked it too casually and the light doesn't come on. He repeats the process, pushing a stiff index finger against the button this time. The light comes on. It's an old kettle. The plastic surface is dull and grey in places where it had once been white. Maurice stands there, wondering how he will fill the two or three minutes while he waits for it to boil. It is at this point that he notices Sandford. He must have followed him in here. His shoes do not squeak. They stand there together on the cheap red linoleum of Aunt Patricia's kitchen floor. Sweat beads Sandford's forehead. His scar is a livid pink.

*

The first Maurice might have been expected to detect anything is about half a second before it happens, as he turns around when his eye is momentarily caught by the sight of the hardened yolk of his breakfast egg plastered thinly across the corner of an unwashed plate. He wonders why he did not put it in to soak, and is telling himself that he will do so while he waits for the kettle to boil, when he glimpses the raising of Sandford's eyebrows, as though unseen hooks attached to the skin of his forehead are being tugged backwards across his scalp. Simultaneously, his lips assume a related shape, the lower being squashed into the upper, the force of their contact pushing out, in a thin bulbous layer, the flesh beneath it where he has, Maurice now notices, neglected to shave. His nostrils flare, his chin disappears into a square of hard, pocked flesh. Maurice has time for a single thought, which is that Sandford is about to faint again, perhaps die this time, and that it seems somehow right, if inconvenient, that it should happen here, in this house, in front of him.

The common trajectory of his facial features, it becomes clear in the next split second, is aligning them with his unfurled right arm, which is flung out behind his back and on the end of which, although he cannot see it until it has travelled a certain distance towards him, Sandford's fist is clasped. Like a discus thrower, he swivels on the ball of his outer foot, channelling the energy from the other parts of his body into the wide arc his right hand is making on its way to a point between Maurice's own cheek and jaw, where it connects with a force Maurice does not feel until he comes to, blinking and disoriented, a few seconds later.

What he can hear is gushing water. It is Sandford, standing at the sink behind him, soothing his bruised hand. Maurice is lying on the floor. It is not a giving surface and the linoleum feels sticky against his cheek. On the other side of his face, he can feel the traces of a ball he must have been in the process of swallowing. But the ball is his own swollen tongue, and what he is swallowing is blood. He has been hauling himself away from the middle of a whirlpool, a huge sucking corkscrew of indiscriminate power. Those concentric circles are everywhere, rotating at dizzying speed in the vortex itself, but slower in the pink and purple windows of the rabbit's kaleidoscopic eye, in his son lumbering round and round the rugby field, in the openings to secrets known only to him, beginning with his wife's round stockinged knee, in the faces with which Patricia surrounded herself where they float, rather, like corks on the ocean. He has paused, exhausted, unsure whether he has the strength to continue hauling himself up, dazed and relieved to find himself in touch with this unmoving floor. He stays there for a minute or two, making no attempt to move anything except his eyes. In spite of the surface, it feels better than trying to lift his head, for when he does so he sees stars. They drift in and out of his vision, dim suspended circles coming and going, large and small, hard and soft, fading to nothing then growing again like slow, silent explosions. They might be the disembodied neurons in his brain trying to reconnect with one another.

Maurice is starting to think again. What does he do now? What should be his next move? He is not a violent man. He has never struck another human being, except on the rugby field, where it doesn't count. As a young man, once he was present at a bar where a fight broke out and had, he will admit, been an enthusiastic spectator although he had never felt the urge to join in. Having grazed, another time, the corner of someone's Ford Falcon in a car park, he found himself confronted by its fist-itching owner, whom he was able to stare down by stepping out of his own car and demonstrating his vastly superior height, five or six inches of it, although he would probably not have done so if the owner had been less small.

The thing is, he has no idea how to proceed. He has never been part of a world where these things happen. Is there a fighters' code of behaviour, a protocol he could follow? Should he be attempting to return the favour, should he be pretending it didn't happen, is there something he is expected to say? And then, what is the form when you open your eyes and find your attacker calmly attending to his own injuries? It is all new ground for Maurice and it does not look as though Sandford is going to help by providing a lead of any sort. He struggles into a sitting position and tries to focus. With some effort, he pulls his double vision together. His tongue hesitates to explore the inside of his mouth for fear of what it might find. His eye aches.

'What was that for?' he hears himself saying.

Sandford does not answer immediately. He emerges from the other side of the kitchen table with a wet cloth which he presses against Maurice's cheek, opening up the fingers of Maurice's own hand so he can hold it in place, much as Maurice had done for him a few weeks before. He should have been a nurse, Maurice thinks. For a moment, he wonders if perhaps the two of them have been attacked by a third person and are now united by their injuries. But he finds he can recall everything quite clearly behind those pullulating circles.

'What do you think it was for, Maurice?' Sandford says, emphasising the 'you' as though he is interested, particularly, in Maurice's opinion on the matter.

Maurice shakes his head, as far as he is able. It's starting to sound like a game. Games are no use. He wants answers.

'Do you think you don't deserve it, Maurice?'

Maurice shakes his head again, not in response so much as to ward off the effect of the questions. His eyes are fully focused now and he is able to take in everything around him. His cheek hurts but the damp cloth feels surprisingly soothing. Sandford is standing up at the sink again, running the tap over his hand. He looks taller, although that could be because Maurice is sitting on the ground.

'I don't know what you're talking about,' he says. The words come out surprisingly easily. He finds himself slurring on purpose, in case Sandford thinks he has not been injured enough. He does this not so much because he is afraid of being hit again as because he has the impulse to elicit his sympathy. Why would he want to do this? he asks himself. It makes no sense, but no less sense than anything else.

'It's a simple question,' Sandford says. 'Do you think you don't deserve it?'

'Yes. I mean, no. I mean – I don't know.'

'Which is it?'

'Yes, no. Why are you asking me this? What's it got to do with you anyway?'

'If I didn't do it, who would?'

'What are you talking about? This is…' He is about to say ridiculous but checks himself. It seems like too many syllables for his mouth.

'It sounds as though you need me to tell you.'

'It sounds as though you're going to, whatever I say.' Maurice winces from the pain these words cause him, for he has spat them out more forcefully than he should, without regard for his bruised jaw. It is not in his interest to be feisty just now.

Suddenly he has a view of himself from above, a figure sitting on this expanse of kitchen floor unable to protect what dignity he has left, and not really concerned about doing so. Sandford is looking down on him from his perch on the chair, shooting down his words with words of his own. He could not explain it, but a balance seems to have been achieved. Maurice is used to setting the agenda. He is not used to being dictated to. The sort of reaction he would expect from himself, even in his current state, is to take control, call the police, press charges; and chuck this person out of his house, out of his life. But he does not even think of doing so. A strange fascination has arisen in him. He wants to see where this is going. He wants to see what Sandford is going to do next. He does not want to fight it. Buried in the layers with which he cloaks himself there is a sense in which he approves of what is being done.

'Is there any reason to tell you, Maurice? I think you already know.'

'If it's about the bicycle,' Maurice says, mentioning the least complicated thing that comes into his mind, 'I'm prepared to admit I was wrong. I should have told you about it as soon as I realised it was yours. I'll compensate you for it, I told you. I'll give you money.'

'All right, Maurice.' Sandford gives a single, confirmative nod, but he is not drawn to say anything further.

'And all the other stuff we got rid of,' he says. 'I don't know why you had it or what was going on but I'll give you money for that as well. I'll give you a fair price for it all.'

Sandford nods again, with a half motion this time. It is as though with these head movements he is operating a pump which is squeezing the words out of Maurice.

'Is it because of Patricia?' he ventures.

'Why are you asking me that, Maurice?'

'She had other relatives, you know, not just me.'

Sandford says nothing. He clasps a wet dishcloth more tightly around his hand. Maurice casts about for something he can do to ensure he is not the next one to speak. He thinks he may be ready to stand up now. His jaw is not as hurt as he had thought. Now he has exercised it by stringing some words together, he finds much of the discomfort has gone. The punch has stunned him, no doubt about that, but nothing is broken. His fingers have found no untouchably tender spots, and apart from a bit of sharp throbbing between his temples his main concern now is the inconvenience of a swollen tongue. He starts to move, but as he does so Sandford speaks again.

'All right,' he says, 'let's talk about Patricia. Why did you say that, when you were standing up there in the church?'

'Why did I say what?'

'You talked about her. You said she was a good woman.'

'What's wrong with that?'

'What did you mean?'

'I didn't mean anything. I meant she wasn't bad. I had to say something.'

'Did you?'

'I was doing the eulogy. Nobody else offered to do it. Why didn't you, if you knew her so well?'

'I wasn't asked, Maurice. You didn't even want me in the car.'

'I didn't know you existed, until then.'

'Did you know anything about her, Maurice?' Sandford suddenly says. 'Did you ever talk to her? Did you ever have a real conversation with her?'

'I had plenty of conversations with her,' Maurice says, remembering those awkward drives when he used to turn the music up to save them both the embarrassment of having nothing to say. 'I used to drive all the way over here to pick her up. No one else did that.'

It is as though he hasn't spoken.

'Did you ever ask her a real question?' Sandford is almost shouting now. He gets down off the chair, pulling it away from the table to make room for himself. The chair's legs scrape discordantly across the lino. Sandford leaves the room.

Maurice feels rooted to the spot in a way he never has before. He has no doubt that Sandford will be meting out more punishment when he returns and the floor is the worst place he could be. For some time, he has no idea how long, he stays down there, physically unable to rise to his feet or even make the first moves towards doing so. It feels quite beyond him to work out which muscles to call upon to start the whole process of standing, or even what sequence of movements he should adopt. For instance, should he roll over and crawl to an upright position through the knees or should he try to push himself up from the heels? Or should he attempt some combination of the two? And should he try to stand unaided or should he use an item of furniture, one of the chairs perhaps, to pull himself up? Indeed, should he simply inveigle Sandford into helping him, and in doing so perhaps reassert some of the control he appears to have given away? These are actions that are normally executed outside thought, not only the movements themselves but in his case also the act of applying his authority. But now he is thinking about them, and the simple act of thinking has set in train a thousand decision points, each with its potential for indecision, of which he appears to have taken advantage to the point where he is now frozen at every turn.

Perhaps Maurice falls asleep for a few seconds, for the next thing he is aware of Sandford is back in the room, this time leaning against the bench top that lines one wall, and Maurice is still on the ground but cradling his head in the crook of his right arm. Sandford has a cigarette in his hand. He lights it with a match from a box Maurice keeps for emergencies next to the fruit bowl. He brings the flame up to his face and stares at it before blowing it out with a puff that is not as deft as might be expected. In the soft evening light, the presence of the flame makes an appreciable difference to the light in the room.

'Is it something to do with my work? Do you have a problem with what I did for a living?'

'We're all entitled to make a living,' Sandford says.

He flicks the used match onto the floor. It lands close to Maurice's face and he catches a brief sulphurous whiff in his nostrils. Once again, he hauls himself into a sitting position.

'We're vital for the health of the economy, you know. Just because we don't produce something you can see. We work much harder than the people that make the tables, you know. We risk a lot more as well.'

'You make a lot more money too,' says Sandford.

'Is that it? Do you resent me for making money? Because if you resent me, you're going to have to resent a lot of other people too. It's the way the world works. You need to get used to it.'

'Oh, I am used to it, Maurice. I'm used to people taking more than their share.'

Maurice does not normally care to justify himself but the words are leaving his mouth before he has a chance to screen them. Seeing himself from afar, he is disconcerted to hear himself saying these things when his normal self would not have allowed this dialogue to continue beyond the first sentence, but here, from where he is lying, it seems somehow part of the natural order of things.

Now at last he has set in motion the chain of events that leads to him being seated on a chair at the kitchen table. It is not so difficult after all. The trick is to not think about it. Ranged in front of him are a folded page of yesterday's newspaper, various items waiting to be washed up from his last meal, a half drunk bottle of shiraz, a lidless jar of coffee, a dishcloth, car keys. There is also Sandford's smoking paraphernalia, resplendently alone, on the cleared half of the table. The front of Maurice's tongue is swollen and pushing against his teeth and the roof of his mouth and the insides of his cheeks. He feels the sweet tang of his own blood with its curled-back edges but it is too concerned with its own trauma to taste it. Upright now, he thinks he sees more clearly. Sandford moves across to the sink. Behind him the late afternoon sun explodes.

'Why should I apologise?' Maurice says abruptly, as though the sun's sudden appearance has inspired a commensurate revelation. 'Why should I apologise for making a living? I had a family to support. Why should I apologise for that?'

Sandford drops his hot cigarette butt into the sink. Even from where Maurice is sitting, he catches the smell of the soaked burned tobacco as it mingles with the pulped vegetable peelings in the plughole. Maurice makes to object but the thought is quickly rolled by more pressing concerns.

'So, I sailed close to the wind at times, but so does everyone. You have to to compete.' Maurice is growing used to his tongue, and the extra care he must take when forming his words. 'Did I love it?' he says. 'Damn right I did. I won't apologise for it!'

'I'm not asking you to apologise, Maurice,' says Sandford. 'I'm not asking you for anything.'

'And Patricia,' Maurice continues, as though Sandford has not spoken, 'she was an independent human being. She made her own choices. I could have ignored her completely, so why should I apologise for what I did do?'

Once again, Sandford has started to roll a cigarette. He is in no hurry this time. He performs all the familiar moves with a contemplative air, as though it is a deliberate ploy to use up time, to draw the words out of Maurice's mouth.

Suddenly, Maurice sees Patricia in this room, sitting at this same table, perhaps in this same chair. She has seen herself through to the end of another day, another day on which she has woken up in the morning, early of course because she doesn't sleep, and immediately embarked on the routines whose only purpose is to give structure to those vast empty days. Breakfast – nothing more than tea and a piece of toast but lovingly prepared, delicately savoured then afterwards cleaned up, the knife, the cup, the plate, scrubbed away down to the last crumb in a ceremony that can sometimes be made to last up to an hour. Now there is only another hour to fill before she can start on her journey down the road to the café where she will meet with Sandford and which, including the journey back, will see her through until lunchtime. As long as she can keep these empty times down to an hour or so, they are easily filled with a little desultory housework, a cup of tea or even, though this is avoided if possible for its vicious reminders of her isolation, a glance at daytime TV. It is important to mark the moment when the afternoon turns to evening, for this is when she has broken the back, so to speak, of her day. Now she can start to let down her guard, she can allow the discipline to lapse, give herself up to a few hours' idleness in front of the TV. It is also the time when she can start to think about dinner, never a complicated meal but nonetheless one whose conception, preparation, eating and cleaning up can be accomplished with an elaboration that is only hinted at by her breakfast routine. And after that, it is once again touching distance to bedtime. He knows how it must have been for her, because this is how it is starting to be for him.

'She never said anything,' Maurice says. 'How can you help a person who never says anything?'

And yet, underneath it all, there is something about Aunt Patricia that he can't help but envy. Is it that unexpected self-possession that allowed her to reveal and conceal as she chose? Or that, from the wrong end of the vast disparity in their lives, she was still able to look at him and laugh? Or perhaps it's that, even in the face of the marginalisation he has now begun to experience for himself, she remained open to creativity, to friendship and love, and was able to get through her life without artifice or self-aggrandisement, without building shrines to the person she wanted to believe she was. When all is said and done, what's most confounded him is her simple capacity to make him think these things.

For the rest of the evening, they sit there in silence. Time is measured by Sandford's regular forays into the tobacco pouch, after which, for five minutes or so, the stale smoked smell is replaced by fresh stuff. Failing light gradually leaches definition from the objects in the room until Maurice rises to his feet and flicks the switch. He blinks. He feels light-headed. He feels no trace of pain in his jaw while it is at rest, but when he tries to talk it sets up an ache which turns into a dull throbbing across his head that takes whole minutes to die down.

That night, there is no discussion about buses, taxis and lifts in Maurice's car. The idea of Sandford going home is not even raised. When Maurice finally drags himself upstairs, Sandford goes up too, laying out the foam mattress that has been propped up inside the cupboard in the main bedroom. He does this with a sense of purpose that speaks of an action performed many times before, squaring it up in his preferred corner of the room and accepting Maurice's offer of a clean towel without a word.

**10**

The person I am sharing a cell with cries himself to sleep every night. He is a family man, wrenched arbitrarily from his wife and three children. I suppose that is why they put us together, two family men. I saw the look of abject relief on his face when they brought him in here and he saw that he was not to be sharing with the bull-necked, tattooed psychopath of his nightmares. I climbed down from my bunk, where I had been reading, stood on the floor and shook his hand. I now realise this was a mistake. I should have presented a less unthreatening front. Such was his relief that he imagined we were to be friends and immediately set about regaling me with all the details of his life – his family, his profession, the unfortunate series of events that caused him to be in here. He has not given me a moment's peace since. Next time I will be more careful. And make no mistake, there will be a next time, and a time after that. I will still be here long after he's gone, greeting the next in my succession of cell buddies.

He killed an old man. It wasn't his fault, he has told me over and over again. He and his wife were at a party, a dinner party in the same mould as I used to attend with my own. It was her turn to drive, his to drink, but partway through the meal she accepted her third top-up of sauvignon blanc and claimed to have forgotten what they had agreed. He had no choice, he said. On the way home, the old codger pulled out unexpectedly in his lovingly maintained Morris Minor. He veered, but not soon enough, and clipped the codger's car smartly on the driver's side. One less glass of wine, a single one, and he would have been in the clear, but as it was he was over the limit and the full wrath of righteous society descended upon him. As long as he behaves himself, he'll be out in six months but this means little to him. His shame and misery overwhelm him. His life is ruined, he says.

'Why me?' he moans.

He actually says this. At first, I used to answer him. I'd make what I thought were consoling noises about chance and the sheer randomness of events. It was true, I would say, that on any given night in this one city there were probably another ninety-nine husbands agreeing to drive home when they had had one glass too many. And out of them, a single one might have an old codger pull out in front of him, and if he did, the codger might move a split second sooner, giving him an extra split second to turn the wheel, which he would manage with ease and drive away leaving no one any the wiser. And every now and then, the codger might pull out at the worst possible time but the husband might, owing to some particularity of the atmospheric conditions, see him a split second sooner and again his evasive action would leave the outcome as it was – the incident forgotten before the night was out instead of reverberating across the rest of his life. And on the occasions when he was unable to avoid hitting the codger, the angle of the vehicles might be such that the damage was superficial, the codger stayed alive and the devoted husband's punishment was nothing more than a fine and the loss of his license. And so on. In other words, I made what seemed to be the only sensible counter to his question – 'Why not you?'

It was a counter I might have found comforting in my current situation, although there had been a time when I would, I imagine, have thought like him. My reasoning afforded him little consolation, tending as it did to reinforce the howl of outrage that he of all people had been singled out for this fate. Now all I can do is try to ignore him. After all, we have all transgressed in our lives and the only reason any of us is in this place is because we have been caught. We can bemoan our luck, our upbringing, the severity of our punishment relative to our misdeed, but in reality it is just a matter of degree. The moment we made the decision to do wrong, we were putting ourselves at the mercy of any series of events that might lead us to be here.

He has never asked me what I am in for. I imagine he thinks it is for some respectable white-collar crime, tax evasion or insider trading or something. Or perhaps he did not dare ask at first, and recognises that we have now been together long enough that he has rather missed his chance. I do not intend to enlighten him. I prefer to keep it up my sleeve, just in case I ever have occasion to demand that extra respect it would surely demand.

I have been here several months now. The precise number, I could not say, in contrast with my cell mate, who is able to calculate, to the nearest hour, the time he has served and the time he has remaining. I lost track of time very quickly, to the point where I could no longer with certainty state the name of the month, let alone the day of the week. I prefer it this way. The measurement of time has no relevance here, except as a form of torture. It is meaningless to state that a day has passed, since there is always another one to take its place. And as each day is much the same as the one that has gone before, there seems little to gain by attempting to distinguish between them. Others, of course, have a different view and would contend that the counting of them is precisely what does distinguish them. They would say that this is the only way to extract meaning from one's time here. But I would say, let meaninglessness run wild! Meaninglessness is reality, and it will find us in the end, wherever we might hide.

I am quite comfortable in my cell. When I first saw it, I thought I would never get used to being cooped up in such a tiny space. It's like living permanently in your bathroom. The whole thing is only slightly bigger than the one in Patricia's house, and it is smaller than the en suite next to the bedroom I shared with my wife. But after a couple of days it ceased to bother me. Within a week or two, I had grown sufficiently accustomed to all the harsh noises and lights to screen them out too. (Not the smells, though. I wonder whether that might come in time.) I would not say I am content but I want for very little. I think I could be content if I had it to myself, but this does not seem to be an option. This enforced intimacy with another person not of your choosing is presumably part of the punishment, although I have heard it said that it is also intended to be a socialising influence, without which some would succumb to various forms of madness. I have a kettle and a sandwich maker and a small fridge. These are important because it means I do not have to use the communal facilities. I spend a large portion of each day thinking about and making sandwiches using the various ingredients I am able to keep in here, cheese and meats and jars of this and that. I make them for both of us, and he is suitably grateful, but I do not allow him to make them for me.

For the most part, my time consists of the same few activities as my life did on the outside. I sleep, I eat, I exercise. I go to my job. The difference is in how I spend the time when I am not doing these things. On the outside, there is a great deal of choice available; in here, there isn't. In some ways, I have found this beneficial. When there is no choice, there is none of the anxiety associated with choosing badly. My life is forced onto narrow tracks from which deviation is just not possible, and there is a certain satisfaction involved in getting through another day without succumbing to the boredom and ennui which are always in the offing.

I have my job in the laundry and I have learned to take satisfaction in performing every aspect of it to the best of my abilities. I have set my standards and I refuse to allow myself to fall short of them. I have discovered the trick of wringing every last drop of fulfilment from even the most menial task. I will not pretend it is preferable to the work I did before but I have found a certain freedom in the very restrictions it imposes. I spend two hours every day at the gym. I have a routine there too from which I allow myself no deviation. Aside from the obvious benefits of being fit and strong in a place like this, the discipline brings another focus to my day. At first, I was afraid I would not be able to sustain an exercise regime without a goal in view – running a marathon or playing another season of rugby or whatever – but again, I have discovered that the discipline itself can be the goal. Anything can be a challenge if you make it so. On the outside, there was always the sense of wanting more – more challenge, more risk, more money – and never finding satisfaction because there was always something else to aspire to. In here, there is nothing to aspire to except the accomplishment of getting through to the end.

Sometimes, our expectations are reduced still further. An example of this is the lockdowns. They seem to occur more or less at the whim of the authorities, the usual excuse being a shortage of staff to keep us under control. On occasions, they have been known to last all day, although usually they are for just a few hours. At lockdown time, we may be confined to our units or, more severely, to our cells. We are unable to do most of the things we normally do to see us through our days. Those of us with routines have them broken and we have to fall back on an even slighter caricature of a real life than the one we have become accustomed to. Thus, for instance, instead of using the gym equipment for exercise, I will improvise using the contents of my cell, pushing against the frame of the bunk bed, running and jumping on the spot, performing callisthenics with the aid of a chair. Unfortunately, I am also forced to endure the TV set they have allowed my cell mate. He never seems to switch it off. I believe he uses it as a sort of opiate, a screen between his mind and reality. Through him, I have become acquainted with the full range of what passes for entertainment on the commercial channels these days. It has improved since I suggested he invest in an earpiece so that he could listen without disturbing me but it is still difficult, in such a confined space, not to be infected by the silent parade of inanity as it flickers across the screen. It also means I am compelled to let him know when I do feel like watching something, which puts me in his debt in a way I would rather avoid.

Lockdowns are the only times my cell mate seems to relax. I believe he looks forward to them. At these times, and also at night, our cell is a cocoon, an extra set of walls within walls. There is no possibility of an unexpected visitor because everybody else is locked into their own cocoons as well. For a time, we are quarantined from the prison's overall air of unease. He puts his feet up and snoozes in front of his TV. I put in my earplugs and read. I pay special attention to my stretches and exercises. We are like a strange parody of a married couple, conversant with one another's idiosyncrasies, vaguely contemptuous in our ease and familiarity. Outside the cell, he considers me his protector. It's not that I would be able to physically look after him, in spite of my working out, it's more that I understand how to carry myself. I have tried explaining to him but he seems unable to grasp the concept. I carry myself quietly, I generally speak only when spoken to, I neither seek nor avoid eye contact – if it comes, I find a quick, silent nod defuses any tension that might be simmering. I never smile. My cell mate's only gambit has been to grow his beard. His hope is that this makes him unattractive and maybe slightly fearsome. To my mind, it also acts as a buffer between himself and the world that is treating him so cruelly, as well as insisting, by a different outward show, that the person behind it is not really him.

When I arrived here, I was given a list of potential jobs and allowed to place them in order of preference. After my obvious first choices of the library and the carpentry workshop, I did not give it a lot of thought and so I found myself allocated to the laundry, which I had placed next on my list. It is not a popular choice but I do not find it disagreeable. I work for three hours in the morning and another three in the afternoon. I am hoping, in the near future, to swap my morning shift for an evening one. This will allow me to return to my unit an hour or two after lockdown each evening, thus lessening the amount of time I have to spend in the company of my cell mate. If I am lucky, he might forge a relationship with one of the other men in our unit, and further reduce his dependence on me.

My job is for the most part hot, smelly and dull but this is alleviated when it is my turn to operate the steam iron. Its purpose is to press sheets, shirts and blankets, not so much for presentation as for storage – pressed flat, twice as many can be fitted on a shelf. I take particular satisfaction in feeding in some creased and rumpled sheet and squashing it almost into non-existence. Another advantage of the job is that I am generally able to perform it in silence. The rattle of the machines and the hiss of the steam make it difficult to carry on a conversation and anyway, neither of the two men who normally work with me is a talker. We are left pretty much to our own devices here and as long as we do our work no one bothers us. Neither of my workmates offers any spark of initiative – indeed one of them appears to be genuinely retarded – and they are happy to defer to me whenever there are decisions to be made. I think that is why we are left alone. The authorities can see that we've got our pecking order sorted out, that we are comfortable with our positions and that I provide enough direction to the other two to get the job done.

For the most part, I try not to get involved in conversations with anybody. I have no interest in making friends and if I wish to pass the time of day, I would much rather do it by myself. One thing that is completely absent from life here is anxiety about social status. When I was young, there was no mortification worse than being outside the group, whether that manifested in having no one to talk to at a party or in not knowing enough people to invite to my own. Even later, when I thought I had left this behind, I can see that a lot of my preoccupations were concerned with a continuing need for acceptance, and that there was always the need to keep at bay the potential for private shame when this did not come about. Now it is just an odd memory.

This is just one of the many social norms, the unassuming causes of stress and anxiety on the outside, that do not apply here. We all mind our ps and qs, both to the guards and to each other. This is the least that is expected, but there is not a great deal more expected either, and the penalty for not doing so tends to be far more direct and peremptory than the subtle ostracism that might be felt on the outside. There is no obligation here to be seen to be part of a group, although this might be considered a wise course of action for other reasons. There are none of those gatherings where people compete for ascendancy in their conversational circles and nobody looks askance if you are on the outer. Society has already looked askance at us and we are no longer subject to its arcane little survival mechanisms. Granted, they have been replaced by others more brutal but once they have been absorbed, there is a certain scope for non-conformity that does not exist on the outside.

This is something I indulge, from time to time, in a mild way, revelling in the knowledge that there will be no consequences. For instance, last Sunday my cell mate was granted a day out to attend some family crisis and I basked in my sudden eleven square metres of personal space. I spent all day lying on my bed, alternating between crossword puzzles and a couple of books. It was behaviour that would never have been countenanced by my wife, or indeed by my former self. Both of us would have considered it a criminal waste of my time. But in here all time is wasted, and you start to understand that it is the same, when all is said and done, on the outside as well. Why should one activity mean any more than any other? I had performed my own version of a lockdown. I wouldn't have minded if I had been shackled to my bed. It would have meant no more than another, a fourth, in the concentric circles of confinement that exist here, after the prison itself, the unit and the cell, none of which has any further meaning for me after the first.

**11**

The next morning, Sandford is already up when Maurice comes downstairs. He is sitting at the table in the kitchen smoking, his tobacco pouch open in front of him, using one of last night's takeaway containers as an ashtray. Maurice counts the remains of at least three smoked fag ends in the yellowish gravy, looking like some exotic, papery herb. He starts to clear up, stacking the plates and cutlery in the sink and stowing the containers back into the plastic bag they came in. His tongue feels thick, rather than swollen, and he can feel the loose skin around the cut on the inside of his cheek, flaked like the appendages of some marine growth. Otherwise, though, his head feels clear, and the tenderness of his bruised jaw is only apparent when it is touched.

The clear light of day provides no revelatory reassessment of Sandford's presence. He is sitting in the same position as last night, wearing the same clothes, even smelling the same, and his presence seems neither more nor less than it should be. This house is more home to him than Maurice could ever claim for himself. Every few hours, he has demonstrated his familiarity with the place in a way Maurice cannot hope to match – this is the correct technique for lighting the stove, this is how they have always prevented the noisy fan in the toilet from starting up when the light is switched on, here is where she sat on her life's last evenings.

'So perhaps it's me that's the intruder,' Maurice says, jokingly.

They go down to the café for breakfast. Is there some need to impress in the way he now mentions that this has become part of his daily routine, or at least a desire to assure him that his example has not been ignored, that he can survive in Sandford's world as well as his own?

Sandford orders the largest and most expensive breakfast on the menu. Maurice orders just coffee for himself but he pays without demur just as he paid for the takeaway meal the night before. They lay claim to Maurice's usual table. Maurice exchanges greetings with the dog-bound women. Once again, the sun dapples the courtyard through the banana palm. They sit. They sip. They wander back to the house.

They seem to have reached a stage where they do not have to talk to each other. In some way Maurice cannot understand, let alone explain, they have come to seem like permanent fixtures in each other's lives. Every corner of the house now holds the smell of Sandford's tobacco and it feels as though it has never smelled any other way. It all seems part of the natural order of things, in the same way as Maurice's thick tongue and his swollen eye. At regular intervals throughout the day, Sandford makes tea, unbidden. Maurice does not try to change his sweet, milky recipe. The thickness coats the inside of his mouth like a protective layer of paint and the sweetness gives him a little boost. He finds this is exactly what he needs, and Sandford is providing it when he needs it.

Almost as though the tea is payment for what he is about to do, each cup he serves generates a new burst of questioning. Again and again, he returns to the subject of human connections, friendship and love.

'Why did you get married?' he asks.

Maurice shrugs. 'Love, I suppose. I loved her.'

'How did you know you loved her?'

Maurice says he just knew, but Sandford will not accept an answer like this. He wants to know what it feels like. He wants it boiled down to a particular sensation, something that could be isolated and examined in a particular part of the body or, failing that, the mind.

'What did you feel, that made you know?' he says.

'I don't know,' says Maurice. 'I wanted to be with her.'

'Is that how you know you love someone?'

'It's one of the ways, I suppose.'

'What are the others?'

'I wanted her physically. I thought about her when she wasn't there.'

Dependence and lust, is this what it comes down to? These are things he has never said to anyone before. He has never even tried to articulate them to himself. Sandford asks Maurice questions as though he is a member of a different species trying to come to grips with something that is outside his domain. He is never quite satisfied with the answers, always digging and probing as though to uncover some underlying root cause from which everything will finally be made clear. It is as though he is trying to find his way to some essence that will forever elude him, because however deeply a question is posed, the answer must be built on assumptions which themselves invite examination.

'What about your son, Maurice, do you love him?'

'Of course. Everyone loves their children.'

'Do they?'

'Everyone that I know.'

'How do you know you love him?'

'I feel protective of him. I'd do anything for him.'

'But what does it actually feel like?'

The image comes to Maurice of his son, the little boy with the dark curls that his mother refused to have cut, keeping them for years until he begged to be allowed to lose them, so he could lose himself among his peers. He felt his son's humiliation almost as keenly as the boy himself. Was that love?

'I felt an intense elation when he was born. I've never felt anything like it since.'

'Where did you feel it?'

'I don't know. In here.' Maurice places a hand on his chest.

'Was that love?'

'I don't know. Perhaps.'

'Do you still feel it?'

'No, but I remember what it was like.'

'Is that why you love him now, because you remember what it was like?'

'No. Yes. Maybe,' Maurice says.

'Who else do you love?'

And so it goes on. Maurice feels pinned down by Sandford's questions, as though he has him physically restrained. He reveals more of himself than he ever knew he had to reveal. He is not normally given to introspection and he is surprised himself by the things he says. Yet they seem to make sense. It is as though a different person is sitting here amidst the empty takeaway containers, unnaturally eager to please his questioner by being as thoughtful and honest with his responses as he can possibly be. Thinking about it later, he wonders if his willingness to do this has something to do with the injury Sandford has inflicted on him. He wonders whether he has been temporarily robbed of his senses.

Now it is evening, and the sun is going down on a full day of the two of them alone in the house together. Once again, some dim notion of social reciprocity begins to stir inside Maurice. Every interaction, he remembers from his long gone days teaching himself the social ropes, demands a response in kind. It is a lesson that has stood him in good stead over many years of trying to place himself in the throng of humanity. It is time to ask Sandford a question or two.

'Tell me,' he says, 'tell me something about yourself. Tell me something about your background.'

Sandford is kneading his tobacco pouch. He continues to do so for a few seconds. Then, with care, he rolls it up and posts it back inside his jacket which is hanging across the back of the chair he is sitting on. He twitches his chin upwards, as though he has made a sudden decision. 'Can I show you something, Maurice?' he says.

'What?' says Maurice.

'We'll have to drive.'

'Where?'

'I don't know the name of the suburb.'

'But you do know how to get there?'

'Yes. I'll direct you.'

'How far is it?'

'I don't know.'

'How long will it take to get there then?'

'That depends how fast you drive, Maurice.'

Before Maurice has a chance to ask him another question, Sandford is on his feet and taking the stairs with unexpected alacrity. He comes down with a bag; blue, canvas, the sort of holdall that might be used to carry tools. With some impatience, he leads Maurice out of the house to where his car is parked. Maurice may not know where they are going but he will be in control of them getting there. He is glad of the excuse to do some driving, to disregard the loss of his parking space for once. It feels like an adventure, with the two of them taking equally crucial roles.

He pushes the button on his key from the other side of the road. The Audi flashes into life, like a dog unexpectedly granted a walk. It is only a few months old and it still retains much of the pristine, moneyed smell of the showroom. The pleasure Maurice takes sinking into the cream leather upholstery has not diminished. Sandford drops his bag onto the back seat before sinking in beside him. The aroma of his tobacco begins to displace the showroom scent. As soon as they start moving, Maurice opens the windows and the city's warm evening air blows across them both. Peak traffic hour has long gone but it is not so late that the streets are clear.

'Left here,' says Sandford, as they approach the first set of lights.

Maurice accelerates around the corner, unnecessarily except for the infusion of pure pleasure afforded by the way the car handles the curve. Sandford sits quietly in his seat, appearing to share Maurice's pleasure – he cannot help but contrast him with his wife who at this point would be  berating him and lunging for the safety strap.

It soon becomes clear that this is not going to be a quick journey. Sandford directs him into a network of side streets from which they emerge, finally, onto one of the main roads that feeds the bridge, which they cross. It is now about eight o'clock and it has been dark for at least an hour. The lanes on the bridge are sparsely filled but the danger in Sandford's directing technique is exposed by the occasional speeding driver taking advantage of the evening freedom.

'Left here,' he says, forcing Maurice to brake and push his way across two not quite empty lanes.

A taxi, forced to brake with him, sounds its horn.

'It would make things a lot easier if you gave me more warning,' Maurice says.

Sandford ignores him. They turn off the main road onto another network of quiet streets. Here the houses all stand by themselves in large yards, most of them fronted by double garages. There are trees everywhere, in the gardens and lining the roads, and there are no people to be seen. The street lighting is weak and no match for the light emanating from the houses themselves. It is an area Maurice knows only from driving his son to rugby matches. Sandford turns him this way and that until it does not seem possible that the most efficient route to any destination could involve so many different streets. He offers no more information beyond his simple directions. He seems to be in a state of deep concentration, a state Maurice does not like to disturb. Normally, faced with such a convoluted route, he would suspect that the person doing the directing has lost their way, but with Sandford the thought does not occur to him. Even if he does not have complete faith in where he is being taken, he has no qualms about getting lost.

Eventually, near the top of a steep, wide road where the verge on both sides is lushly grassed, Sandford tells him to pull over. He removes his seat belt and twists round so that he is looking back down the other side of the road. 'Go back a bit,' he says, after studying the scene for a few seconds.

Maurice lets off the handbrake and they roll a few feet.

'Stop,' he says.

Maurice follows what he takes to be Sandford's line of sight. This is a street of large, modern houses, and the one they are looking at is one of the biggest. It is not unlike the house Maurice and his wife had built after they were married. The whole property is fronted by a thick sandstone wall topped with decorative black railings inside which a row of firs has been planted, so the house itself is only partly visible. What

Maurice can see is a large, well windowed building whose brick facade has been cleanly rendered in sand. The house is set well back from the front of the property, behind a substantial lawn in the centre of which stands another fir, mature this time and much taller than the house. All this is clearly visible because there seems to be a light on inside every window and it streams across the lawn and the driveway, into the flower beds and over the brittle roots of the big tree.

There are two entrances to the property; on the low side a driveway leading, no doubt, to a three-car garage, and on the high side, closer to where they sit, a footpath. Both are served by stout iron gates attached to solid posts. In the right hand one of each, an intercom light glows quietly.

'I take it we've arrived,' Maurice says.

Sandford nods, keeping his eyes fixed on the house.

'What are we doing? Who lives here?'

'Be quiet please, Maurice. There's no need to talk.'

'At least tell me what we're doing here. Are we going in or what?'

'We're not doing anything. We're waiting.'

Maurice does not normally accede to someone else's unelaborated commands, but he has acceded so far and it seems wasteful to stop now. He had expected the drive to take them across, perhaps, a suburb or two, but Sandford has succeeded in directing him to the other side of the city. At some point, it became apparent that he had placed himself completely in his hands. Although it is the last thing he would have expected, in a strange way Maurice has relished doing this, and he has found himself excited, in a way that is quite new to him, by the resulting feelings of abandon. It's a foreign landscape, this ceding of control, and it is drawing out strands of his being he would not have known existed. He says nothing more. For the next few minutes, he watches the house over his shoulder. Apart from the lights, there is little sign of life inside – no sounds, no movements at the windows, nothing except for what might be the faint reflected flicker of a TV, briefly, in a corner of one of the downstairs windows where there is a small gap in the hedge.

Amazingly, he must now fall asleep for a few seconds. He has had the certain feeling that they are in a place far from this and that he has been freed from the burden of ever making a decision again and that this, in spite of all appearance to the contrary, is the correct order of things. It's been like sinking into a soft feather bed.

Now he is alert again to what is in front of him. Sandford is rummaging on the seat behind him, looking for something in his bag, causing the car to shake. This is what has woken Maurice. He glances up in time to see one of the sensor lights go on atop the smaller entrance's sentry post. The gate opens with a dim metallic squawk.

First in view is a dog, sleek and solid with a short stub of tail. It is much like the one Maurice had in the early days of his marriage, a mastiff of some sort. It emerges to the full extent of its lead, sniffing on the ground in eager circles. The lead tautens behind it. Maurice feels a hand on his shoulder.

'Get down,' Sandford whispers.

Without demur, Maurice lowers his head to window level. (For some minutes after this, he continues to feel the claw-like imprint of Sandford's hand on his shoulder.) He watches, trembling slightly, as the figure on the other end of the lead emerges. It is a man, rakishly balding, dressed – white polo shirt, pressed blue shorts and sockless boat shoes – as though he has just stepped off a yacht, the uniform of the wealthy in casual mode, a look favoured by Maurice himself not so long ago. With his free hand, the man is holding a phone to his ear. This commands so much of his attention that he finds the lead momentarily entangled with the gate and is forced into a few moments' graceless untwisting before shepherding the dog through for a second time. Re-establishing the handset against his ear, he looks both ways along the road, seemingly undecided which direction to take, before turning to his left and walking away from them, down the footpath along the front of his property while the dog, fully engaged by the traces of recent visitors to a lone sapling on the grass verge, waits until wrenched by the tautened lead before giving up and trotting away. The hazy glow from a lone street lamp allows

Maurice to observe all this with ease, but at no stage does the man appear to notice their presence.

While this is taking place, Sandford continues fishing in his bag. Maurice is only dimly aware of what he is doing as the bag is on the seat behind him. Sandford grunts and breathes heavily. Then he settles back down in his seat, causing the car to rock with a sudden vigour that would surely have drawn the eye of a more attentive dog walker. Maurice hears a deep, exanimate click.

It is a noise that seems to draw into it all the other sound waves inside the car, a vortex of sound consolidating them into this lonely echo which now fills up the space between them. Maurice turns his head. Sandford is twisted into his seat, half kneeling, left leg pushed against the gearstick, left foot suspended above the thick plush floor mats. In the gap between the headrests, both his hands are now clasped together on the ends of straightened elbows. But there is nothing supplicatory about this gesture. Sandford is holding a gun.

'What…?'

This is as far as he gets with his question. For ten, fifteen, twenty seconds, he simply watches, while every muscle freezes. The line from the gun's short barrel, down his hands and his denim sleeves, starts at Sandford's eyes. His head is even lower than Maurice's, barely able to see over the window's bottom edge. As he follows his target, this line moves slowly to his right; the gun, the hands, the arms and the eyes all moving as a single entity. The pale eyes narrow and focus.

Sandford is completely silent apart from his breathing, which slowly encroaches into the space made vacant by the fading click, and which finds a more physical manifestation in the smoked tobacco smell now permeating the interior of Maurice's car. The figure walks briskly down the outside of the neighbouring property before disappearing into the shadow of some bushes, the dog now trotting obediently by his side with nimble, economical movements. They show briefly as slight agitations in this shadow, then they are no longer there at all, lost to the dip in the road. The whole process takes no more than a few seconds, yet such is the sharpness of Maurice's senses during this time that it feels as if they have been watching him for several minutes. All the different strands of tension are hostage to the final squeeze on the trigger and the firing of the gun; but it isn't fired. As they disappear, Sandford relaxes, his elbows withdraw and bring the weapon back towards him. He turns and sits up in his seat, unfolding his knees and resting it on his lap. Then he closes his eyes.

'Let's go,' Maurice says at last.

He turns the key. The engine throbs quietly. Sandford places both hands across his lap, covering the gun, and keeps them there for the rest of the journey. He does not speak a word until they walk through the front door.

*

'So,' Maurice says, 'are you going to tell me what all that was about?'

He has spent the whole of the return journey in a state of barely suppressed excitement. His heart, which started racing as soon as he saw the gun, continues to bubble and froth as though the spillage of adrenalin has not been contained. Sandford, though, sits there in a state of seeming serenity, as though his actions have loosened some pressure valve inside his head. Maurice had wanted to start talking sooner but, because he hardly knew where to start, he found himself waiting for Sandford to provide a prompt of some sort – to put away the gun, to roll a smoke, to sigh, to cough…anything. But he does nothing at all. He has not made a sound or moved a muscle for the entire journey, and by the time Maurice realised he was not going to, his waiting had become a habit from which he was unable to extricate himself. Maurice was in his hands. For those thirty minutes as they drove back across town, he would have done anything Sandford told him to. He also realises that he had really wanted him to fire the gun.

'I'm dying for a cup of tea,' says Sandford.

Maurice goes to the kitchen and fills the jug. While he waits for it to boil, Sandford rolls a cigarette on the dining table. By the time he comes out with the tea, he has lit up and is blowing his hot, sweet smoke across the room. Maurice finds him a saucer to use as an ashtray.

'Thanks, Maurice,' he says.

Maurice feels absurdly glad to hear his name being used. He takes his own place at the table, among the drifting clouds of smoke. 'Can I see it?' he says.

Without removing the cigarette from his lips, Sandford reaches into his lap, where the gun still resides. He slides it out and hands it to Maurice across the table, holding it so the barrel is pointing away from them both. It is a revolver, sleek and squat around its fat little chamber. Maurice holds it. It feels satisfyingly weighty. He runs his thumb down its lines and across the dimpled bullet vault. There is not a flaw in its blue metalled body. It gleams as though it has just come off the production line. Even the grip, which is finished in varnished, honeyed wood, shows no wear. It is a marriage of function and form, perfect in what it is. He finds himself suppressing a gasp. It's a thing of beauty.

'Is it loaded?'

Sandford nods. Maurice stops staring into the round black hole. He lets it rest on the palm of his hand. There it is, with its unarguable capacity to transcend the ordinary. He is afraid he might find himself following the impulse to use it before he has had the chance to check himself. He places it back down on the table. Sandford immediately picks it up, wraps it in its protective cloth and returns it to the bag, which is on the chair next to him. Here they sit for a moment, on either side of the table, nursing their cups of tea. Maurice has sugared his own this time, three spoons, well stirred. He has held guns before, even fired them, but they have been shotguns and rifles, designed for country use. He has never held one like this, one that is designed for the killing of a person.

'Where did you get it?' he says.

Sandford shrugs. 'I know someone.'

'Have you ever used it?'

'Have I ever shot anyone, you mean?'

'Yes, I suppose so.'

'No.' He says this without shaking his head.

Maurice wonders what it is like to train a gun on another person, to hold their life in your hands, to contemplate the prospect of snuffing it out with a squeeze of your finger. Is it possible that the impulse, the temptation, would be too strong?

'Who was that man?' he asks.

'My brother,' says Sandford.

## 12

Now Sandford starts to talk. He paints a picture of his home as a child, of brothers and sisters, a mother with rippling chins issuing commands from her chair in the kitchen, a father who is mostly invisible when he is not on a tractor somewhere.

Sandford is a middle child, with sisters above him and a brother below. As children, their great aim in life is to please their mother. Love is bestowed and withheld at her whim, and it is hard to know in advance what might bring about one or the other. In fact, from one day to the next, it is quite possible for the same action to bring about both. He describes a woman who fosters a state of intense competition among her children in their efforts to please her. Her love, when it comes, is all-enveloping, her withdrawal of it is cold, sudden and capricious. He describes the feeling of being in her favour, the sense of it, as he nestles into her folds; it is the resolution of all his anxieties, with a vague, uneasy under-knowledge that there is nothing he can do to make it last.

When Sandford is eleven, the defining event of his life takes place. It is a mealtime, around the table in the big farmhouse kitchen. His sisters have already made themselves useful, laying the table and placing in front of their mother the big bowl of stew she has prepared that afternoon, and from which she will serve them, using an old pewter ladle. It has been a good day, Sandford remembers, and he has had to repress the irrational euphoria which always bubbles beneath the surface at such times. It is hard to explain, he tells Maurice, but a single word of kindness from his mother seems to unleash in him a corresponding delirium, a feeling that he can get away with anything. On this occasion, she directs a rare smile his way as she commences ladling, a favour he takes to indicate he now has sufficient credit banked to do some drawing down.

He is not one for hoarding such credit. He casts around for something to spend it on and his eye falls on the bowl that belongs to his younger brother, newly filled and steaming. While his brother is looking the other way, he manages to insinuate his own spoon into the bowl and come away with a morsel of meat and gravy that he eats without, he thinks, being spotted by anyone else in the room. Then he tries again.

This time, as expected, he is not so successful. A beady-eyed sister spots him from across the table and draws shrieked attention to his misdemeanour. This alerts the brother, who adds his own howls to the protests. It is Sandford's view, in retrospect, that his mother's subsequent reaction has more to do with the screams of his siblings than the original crime, as she has always seemed peculiarly sensitive to noise and they all know to keep their distance when she has one of her 'heads'.

'If you can't behave at the table, you can go and eat in the shed,' she says to him.

Sandford's misfortune, at this point, is his failure to grasp, immediately enough, the change in atmosphere. The unusual good humour with which his mother commenced her ladling has led him to believe he has the leeway of one more transgression before she turns. Nudged by the imp on his shoulder, he again lunges for the bowl over the protective arm that his brother has now thrown across the table between them. There is a brief skirmish, some gravy is spilled and Sandford giggles and withdraws, but not before being startled by a quick sudden shadow between him and the light in the middle of the ceiling. He looks up. There, hovering over the table, dripping yet more gravy onto the cloth, shudders the big pewter ladle, on the end of it his mother's hand, leading, by way of her arm, to a face now framed by the thunderous expression his calculations have led him to believe he will avoid.

'Out!' she cries. Take your dinner and eat in the shed!'

They all stare.

'With the rabbit!' smirks his brother.

Sandford looks up. She is still pointing with the ladle. He knows better than to disobey this time.

The shed, reached by a brick path from the house's back door, does not seem such a terrible place to be. It is part of a larger outbuilding on one side of which is a garage and on the other a dank little room with a sink in which has formerly stood a washing copper. The shed itself is about six feet by six, with the rabbit in its raised cage on one side of the door, a pair of straw bales on the other and a myriad of garden implements between. Buckets, coils of wire and rope, bags filled with nuts and bolts, hats, gardening clothes and smaller tools hang from nails driven into almost every visible section of the exposed wooden joists. There is no light in the shed itself but it is possible to borrow small amounts by switching them on in the adjoining rooms. Sitting on the bales between the soft covered walls with the warm, rabbity smell in his nostrils, Sandford feels almost cosy.

The rabbit lives in a large hutch that the children take turns to clean out each week. They do this by removing the rabbit, raking the fouled straw to one end of the cage, then opening a hinged flap in the floor to let it all drop out. The hutch was designed and constructed by their father who, on the rare occasions when he is not working, invents projects for himself that get him out of the house. It is one of a series of constructions that include a caged vegetable garden, various items of play equipment, sheds, pathways and even extensions to the house itself. As a farmer, he does not approve of rabbits but is prepared to make an exception if it gives him the chance to exercise his joinery skills. The rabbit started off small and brown but has now grown fat and is almost black in places. It is the only survivor of a litter that was discovered by one of the neighbouring dogs on an expedition Sandford made with his sisters and some of the nearby children to the farthest reaches of the adjoining property. They carried back five or six of them, with fantasies of building their own rabbit colony in an abandoned shed. One of the baby rabbits was dead before they got it home and most of the others died soon after. But this one did not. It watches Sandford now, loping gently across the face of the cage and lifting itself occasionally to sniff the air with its ever-twitching nose.

Sandford describes how he finished his dinner in the half-light, seated on the straw bales, watched by the rabbit. The shed has been a punishment often threatened, seldom used. On the only other occasion this has happened to him, one of the others was sent out soon after to collect his plate and bring him back. Sandford waits, but no one comes. From the kitchen comes the occasional sound of voices, then plates in the sink, then nothing. Eventually, judging that the term of his punishment must be up and that he must have been forgotten about, he picks up his bowl and makes his way back into the house. In the kitchen, all is now quiet. He creeps past the lounge room where his parents are watching TV, and into the bedroom he shares with his brother, who is still awake.

'You're not allowed in here!' his brother pipes up from the darkness,

Evidently there has been some discussion in his absence. He gets out of bed, intending to go and tell their mother. Sandford is bigger and stronger than his brother. He twists his arm up behind him and marches him back. He threatens him with further violence if he says anything.

The next day all seems back to normal. They get up, have breakfast and go to school. One of their morning rituals is to go into their mother's room and wish her goodbye before leaving the house – she never rises until after they've all left. Sandford is not sure what he should do, in view of what must have been said at the dinner table. He decides she would be more likely to be angry with him for not saying goodbye than for coming back into the house without permission. He goes in to her. Everything seems normal. She accepts his kiss and he leaves for school with his brother. On the way, his brother tries to resurrect the subject but he silences him with more threats. In retrospect, he thinks this might have been his mistake.

When the family sits down to eat that night, his brother once again draws attention to some misdemeanour. Sandford is unable even to describe what it is. It might well have been wholly imagined, concocted out of nothing to make trouble for him. Whatever it is, it works.

Their mother crashes her serving implement down on the table and declares that she is not going to allow a repeat of the night before. 'Get out!' she yells. 'Go and eat your dinner with the rabbit, and don't come back!'

Sandford pushes back his chair and walks a gauntlet of silence to the back door. He returns to the shed and sits down on the straw. It is summer, so it's not yet cold, but a lot more of the day's warmth has disappeared from the air compared to the day before. He is wearing shorts, and the straw pricks his legs.

After an hour or so, his father comes out with some blankets. 'You've made your mother very angry,' he says, as though this is the only factor of relevance.

Sandford has to walk round to the garage in order to turn off the light. The straw bales are too small for him to be able to recline across them comfortably. After some experiment, he finds that the best way to maximise the surface area for sleeping is to position them at a slight angle to one another. The straw still pricks him through the blankets. During the night, he hears the soft thumping of the rabbit as it moves in its own straw. He also hears the rustlings of other creatures on the ground, just beneath his face.

In the morning, he is woken by his brother, delivering his school clothes. Still Sandford does not grasp what is happening. He goes into the kitchen and eats his breakfast. After this, he goes into his bedroom to pick up something he needs. His sister sees him in there. She looks surprised but does not say anything. Then Sandford goes in to his mother's room.

He finds her sitting up in bed as usual, propped up by an arrangement of pillows, hair across her forehead still matted from sleep, all the random contours of her upper body covered thinly by her nightie. Even from the door he can smell the familiar smell, the intense night time smell of his mother. Sitting beside her with one foot on the floor is his brother. Sandford recognises the same startled expression, hastily concealed, as he comes into the room. He takes a couple of steps towards the bed. The curtains are drawn back and the room is flooded with unrelenting light.

His mother does not look up, but she stops what she is doing. 'What is he doing in here?' she murmurs to Sandford's brother. She places the accent on the word 'doing', as though to imply that she has no particular objection to his presence but is genuinely unaware of its purpose, as though this is merely the latest activity in a series she has never been able to understand.

Sandford describes his mother's action, or inaction, as 'blanking' him. Until this moment, he says, it has never occurred to him that he might not be loved. He stands there for a long time, but she does not look up. She starts to pet his brother again. His brother continues to stare. Eventually, Sandford withdraws and makes his way, by himself, to school.

To Sandford, this is his paradise lost. All the yearning, all the sense of loss, is focused on the routine of saying goodbye to his mother before school. Every day now, as he puts on his clothes in the shed, or sneaks into the kitchen to find milk for his cereal, he is acutely, physically aware of what is no longer his. Every day now, he imagines the chewed bread smell of his mother, his face burrowed into her damp folds, the feel of their rise and fall as she breathes. He knows that on the other side of the wall this is all being made available to his brother. Once or twice, he even pushes through the hydrangeas at the side of the house, intending to climb up to the window and catch a glimpse of what he is missing. But when the time comes to look through, he finds only torture in the idea of what he might see, and he is not able to bring himself to place his foot on that part of the wall from which he might heave himself up to the level of the window. He imagines his brother, disturbed in the middle of what should be his, getting up and crossing the room to draw the curtain against him. He imagines this so intensely that he cannot, now, be certain that it did not really happen. Most of all he remembers his brother's face, not meeting his own as he walks towards the window, pulling the curtains as though Sandford is just part of the light, shining unpleasantly for a spell, momentarily disturbing the intensity of his experience in the folds of their mother's love.

Sandford is not allowed back into the house. The arrangement is quickly accepted by the rest of the family and incorporated into their routines. At mealtimes, for instance, he has to wait at the back door while one of his siblings brings out his plate. He eats in the shed or, in fine weather, out in the yard somewhere, then places it in a spot next to the door for someone to pick up. Sometimes he hears them arguing inside over whose turn it is. He remembers similar arguments over the rabbit. They are not actually forbidden to talk to him, but they do so less and less.

After a few nights, when it has become clear that his stay in the shed is not going to end soon, his father makes more space for him by moving all the tools out into the garage next door. He brings him a thin foam mattress and fixes up a light on an extension cord. He offers to move the rabbit but Sandford prefers it to stay.

'Don't worry,' he says, 'we'll soon have you back in the house.'

There is no sense that this is a decision his father can make on his own. It is accepted that, like a small country at an international negotiating table, he will bring to bear whatever influence he can, in the full knowledge that nothing will actually happen without the backing of one of the major players. His mother Sandford rarely sees. She spends most of her waking hours sitting in one of her chairs. She hardly ever goes outside. (Sandford reckoned that, with the cooperation of the rest of the family, he could have resumed his former position in the house. The only thing his mother would have needed to know about were mealtimes, and he felt he could have insinuated himself back into these if the rest of them had been prepared to treat his presence as normal.) He makes several more attempts to sleep in his own bed, once even managing a full night there. But his brother, sensing an opportunity to eliminate a rival for his mother's attention, refuses his pleas to keep quiet, and now he simply laughs at his threats. Gradually it becomes clear that Sandford's banishment from the house is permanent.

In time, his father builds a new shed, with a floor and insulation, which he makes comfortable with a bed and a cupboard for his clothes and most of the other trappings of a young boy's bedroom. His father has built it out of kindness but to Sandford this is the worst thing that could have happened. While he slept in the other shed, with the rabbit, on the straw, he was able to believe that this was a temporary arrangement, that any moment it would be over and he would find himself back in the house once more. Now it seems to be officially confirmed that this is never going to happen, that he will never get his place back. This shed becomes Sandford's place and gradually it becomes part of the family mythology that it has been his choice to live in it. He moves the rabbit in with him.

Love is something he has never really thought about. It has certainly never been anything to doubt. If someone had asked him to describe it, he would have pinpointed it as something in the folds of his mother's flesh, something in the scent emanating from her pores when she swallowed him in one of her embraces. Even now, he can close his eyes and imagine it. He can feel the dampness against his cheek of her soft, perspiring flesh behind the thin veneer of her dress. He can even hold the warm, yeasty smell in his nostrils, feel the rough seams of the material against his own skin as she moves her vast body around him. She likes to have a child or two on her as she sits in her chair, although sometimes, without warning, she will push them away and dismiss them. Sandford remembers the feeling of privilege when he was granted the right to climb up and be the focus for her love. Although there was always the chance that he would have to wait his turn or that his place would be usurped, temporarily, by one of the others, there had never been a moment when he doubted he was loved.

*

Sandford has had no contact with any of his family since the night he simply walked away, got on a train to the city and never went back. As a young man, his brother moved here too and Sandford started to observe, from afar, the progress of his career. He describes the shared houses near the beach, the friends, the partying, the various jobs he takes as he finds his feet. Every now and then, Sandford does some detective work. He positions himself with a view of the house where his brother lives, or somewhere else he knows he is going to be, and he sits there for hours watching the comings and goings. In this way, he is able to build up a picture of the life his brother is leading.

One day, Sandford notices, he starts leaving his house in a suit. He has a job at the Futures Exchange. Sandford describes how his brother's bearing changes. He stands taller, he walks with more purpose, he surveys the world around him as though from a greater height. He has his hair cut short and combs a careful parting. He is working long hours now and his leisure time is spent drinking with other traders in pubs near the exchange. Sandford watches the group and the way they jostle for ascendancy. His brother is doing well here too.

'He bought a car,' Sandford says. 'A new one. Red. A bit like yours.'

'An Audi?'

'I don't know. It had those tiny seats at the back. And one of those roofs you can open up. It had a number plate – GO4IT. I used to think it said GOAT.'

'Probably just what happened to be available,' says Maurice remembering his own youthful flirtation with personalised number plates. He is impressed by the progress of Sandford's brother. He wants to understand it in monetary terms, so he can compare it with his own.

Now Sandford finds it easier to keep tabs on his brother. All he has to do is look out for his car. More often than not now, there is a female form in the passenger seat. Sometimes the same one appears often enough for Sandford to start recognising her but mostly they are something of a blur, each one interchangeable with the one before. And still he does not approach his brother in any way.

'Surely he must have noticed you by now?' Maurice says. 'Surely he must have known you were here?'

'No,' Sandford shakes his head. 'He wouldn't have recognised me anyway. He hadn't seen me since I was a kid.'

'Even so, the same figure turning up over and over again – he must have suspected something.'

'I'm pretty good at hiding. And he's not very observant.'

'But didn't you want to meet him?'

'No, Maurice. I thought I did, then I realised I didn't.'

Now his brother moves out of the share house and into an apartment closer to the city. It's on the eighth floor, as Sandford discovers by inspecting the names on the buzzers, and must therefore have a view out over the harbour. At this time, his own accommodation consists of a succession of cheap boarding houses. Once or twice, he finds himself without anywhere to go. He is vague when Maurice asks him how he supports himself, saying only that he does things for people he knows. His brother, he reckons, spends five years living in this apartment and working at the Futures Exchange. He changes his car several times, but keeps the number plate. The girlfriends begin to last longer. The final one – the least attractive in Sandford's opinion, dark and angry-looking – moves in with him. The number plate disappears. Sandford sees him less and less. The attraction of following his progress has dissipated now it is clear that he is never going to confront him. Still, he derives a strange comfort from the knowledge of his brother's presence in the same city.

It is for this reason that the quiet devastation, to which Sandford alludes when one day it becomes apparent to him that his brother has disappeared, does not come as a complete surprise to Maurice. Sandford is, of course, quite used to the idea that sightings of his brother are subject to all sorts of variables, that he might spot him in some regular haunt time after time only to not see him at all for several weeks. Now, though, he has not seen him for months. He appears to have moved, both from his apartment and from the Futures Exchange. His wife, whose place of work Sandford has also occasionally monitored, has also moved. Outside the simple expedient of looking him up in the phone book, Sandford can think of no way of tracing his brother. But the new phone book comes out once a year and for the moment his brother is only there under his old address.

'Why didn't you ask someone else in your family?' Maurice says.

He does not answer.

'So how did you find him again?'

Now Sandford comes as close as he ever comes to a smile. 'I waited until the new edition came out. I looked up his name and there he was, at a new address on the north shore. Of course I couldn't be certain it was him but there aren't that many M. Sandfords in the book and he was the only one that had moved.'

Sandford goes up there straight away. He is rewarded by the sight of his brother and his wife at work in the front yard of the house they have just seen, in a mess of building materials. They appear to be building a front wall to their property. Sandford has to be more careful now when he wants to spy on them, as a lone figure on the street up here tends to stand out in a way he would not in other parts of the city. He makes most of his visits at night so he can remain in the shadows as they have just done. They have a child, he discovers now, a toddler he notices as he peers from a distance into one of the well lighted rooms, staggering around in a tiny pair of dungarees.

'Your nephew,' Maurice says, 'or niece.'

'Yes,' he says as though – and Maurice can well believe it – he has not contemplated this before. 'Yes, I suppose so.'

'And what about the gun,' says Maurice. 'Were you going to shoot?'

'I wasn't intending to. But I was closer than I thought I'd be. It suddenly seemed so simple – the difference between my finger being here,' he cocks his finger and squeezes an imaginary trigger, 'and here.'

'So you could have done it?'

'I just wanted to see what it was like,' Sandford says. 'I wanted to have him there, on the other end of it. Just for once. It made me feel good, Maurice. It felt as though the world was doing what I wanted for a change.'

# 13

My new cell mate is a youngster, sent down for some time-honoured combination of drugs, drink and driving. He did not mean to kill anyone, he assures me, although his patterns of behaviour suggest it was pretty well his destiny to do so. (My weepy friend was released, his sentence suddenly and dramatically reduced. He did not say goodbye. I do not miss him.) I think they have put him in with me in the belief that I will act as some sort of mentor, that this is a kid who is still a step away from being a lost cause. I am prepared to do this. He is, after all, only a few years older than my own son. Considering what I am in here for, I would not have considered myself a suitable person to play this role, but I suppose it is possible that they look upon it as some sort of temporary aberration. Aside from that – and it's a big aside, I grant you – I am, by most objective measures, a person of unimpeachable character, well suited, if anyone here is, to the task of guiding a not quite hopeless case back onto the straight and narrow. The other fellows in my unit seem to have a similar view. I have noticed, more and more, when we sit around chewing the fat after lockdown, how they defer to me for an opinion when something presents itself for dispute, whether it is a matter of simple fact or perhaps a view on the rights and wrongs of some particular behaviour or perhaps just an insight into the workings of the world. The one I inhabited, after all, is one of which most of them have no experience. Perhaps I flatter myself, but I think they look upon me as something of a sage.

It was not always this way. When I first came into the unit, I was viewed with a suspicion that was close to hostility. Don't tell me there is no concept of class in this country! They sniffed me out at once, marked me as a blow-in from some outer social orbit, and treated me accordingly.

This treatment ranged from belligerent refusal to converse to the instinctive reticence whereby a man saves himself from humiliation at the hands of his superiors. It did not help, I suppose, being followed everywhere by that cell mate of mine. In their minds, we must have seemed like a pair, a couple, a two for the price of one deal in which there was no avoiding the hanger-on. In their eyes, I would have been just as responsible for his timid refusal to engage as he was and he, no doubt, for whatever unprepossessing qualities resided in myself. While I was shackled to my unwanted twin, it would have been hard for any of them to do what people invariably do when thrown together in a group – to assign me my proper place in their strict but mysterious pecking order. This was something that had no outward manifestation and would never have been explicitly discussed, but it was an essential component of all our interactions with each other. In some way, I think it boils down to an understanding of how you will react under any given set of circumstances. This in turn allows us to understand who we can count on for what. This might be different for each of us, but we are all united in our need to classify our fellows. Conjoined twins make this all the more difficult in that the responses of each of them might be dependant on or affected by the actions of the other. To express it mathematically, a squaring occurs between the observer and the observed. Now, unshackled, I was an individual, a single unit, no matter how abstruse my demeanour might be, who was observable without the intervention of any numerical prism.

One by one, I have seen them assign me my place, and as this occurs, I notice a commensurate relaxation, an inward sigh of relief at the ticking of the box, at the confidence that I have been assigned to the realms of the known. It was my crime that brought me their respect. As I said, they all treated me with caution at first, wariness to the point of truculence. When they found out what I was in for, they started a certain guarded circling, scratching at some of the more obvious openings to see if I was, in fact, one of them. When they didn't find anything, they decided I might as well be.

The youngest of them, and they are all younger than me, might never have met someone from my walk of life, and their sole experience of houses, even suburbs, like the one where I lived might only have been gained illicitly. Our two young lads are not long out of school but their faces bear the shadows of men ten or more years older. It is only in their eyes that their youth can be discerned – a deadness that arrived before experience – and in their unbought swagger. They were marked out from birth, these boys.

The others are older, they've seen it all, and their attitude towards me is marked by a refusal to be impressed, both by who I might be and whatever I might have done. I have gladdened them immeasurably by my failure to conform to type, by not being aloof, arrogant or overbearing. It being my natural inclination to be all these things, I feel I have Sandford to thank for my new found ability to keep them in check. My life could have been very difficult if I had not. Before I came here, my view of prison was dominated by my random digestion of newspaper articles and half-watched TV shows, from which I imagined I was to be propelled into a netherworld of man-beasts with their own impenetrable codes from which I would be forever excluded. I imagined the violence that would follow them like an aura, and their general impermeability to reason. I imagined isolation too, but as an option this seemed preferable to a life lived under the shadow of sweaty, bull-necked psychopaths. If I had been allowed to choose solitary confinement, I would have done so.

I would be wrong to say that none of this came to pass. In the communal areas, the dining hall for instance or the large, dusty yard, the threat always seems to be there. I see the bull-necks ruling their roosts, I feel the tension simmering, I am careful not to make eye contact, I am careful to maintain my warily feigned indifference. If eye contact cannot be avoided, I have found a slow, grave nod elicits the appropriate measure of respect while implying my own preparedness to honour whatever rights my would-be intimidator is claiming for himself.

Inside the unit, though, it is different. We are like a sports team, in a way, all of us with a vested interest in maintaining balance and order.

Nobody wishes to jockey for a position they would then be obliged to spend all their time defending. All we really want is to be left in peace. The unit is the nearest thing we have to a home. For the two youngsters, it could be the nearest thing they've ever had. I cannot imagine it isn't something like this in other units, although I have heard it is not. Others, I have heard, are a microcosm of life outside, with certain individuals forever asserting their dominance while the rest compete for their favour, all the while on the lookout for that opening or alliance that might give them their own crack at top doggery. This is not to say we don't have tensions. Just the other day, the kids got into a fist fight and, much in the manner of footballers calming down their hot-headed colleagues for the good of the team, we pulled them apart. They are now best of friends once more. I was surprised, although perhaps I should not have been, by how easily they submitted when we became involved, by the speed with which they went from looking for weapons to utter docility. My fellow puller-offer, the only one here close to my age, gave them a screaming lecture in which he enunciated, in a stream of pithy mono-syllables, his overriding desire for a quiet life and his preparedness to in-capacitate in its pursuit. He was speaking for us all when he said this, declaring what amounts to our unit's philosophy. So far we have been lucky. All our arrivals, since my own, have acceded to this point of view. Nobody has felt it worth his while to rock the boat.

We are the only fathers in the unit, he and I, or at least we are the only ones who know the names of our children. We had a conversation about this once, in which he expressed his hopes for his sons, who live with their mothers in two different states. His hopes are modest, but heartfelt, amounting only to a desire that they not follow in his footsteps. His mantra is that he tries to see them as often as he can but it became clear to me, after a few minutes' talk, that this seldom happened. In the case of the youngest, it was unclear whether he had ever even set eyes on him.

I haven't seen my own son since my arrest. It's a long way for him to come – at least that is what I said to my fellow parent, even though it isn't, it's only an hour or so in the car. But the truth is that his mother doesn't want him to and even if she did, I think it is the last thing he would want. He already has the mortification of being the only one at his school with a father behind bars, although, so far is it outside the experience of any of his peers that I can see the possibility, for a boy without his horror of being different, of turning this into a source of prestige.

My one regular visitor is my sister, the younger of the two. She brings me things – biscuits, cakes, meals. Sometimes I share them with the others in my unit, but mostly I don't. It doesn't do to be too eager to please. To her, I am providing the focus and sense of drama which is missing for her during what seems to be a lull in her own life. She is impressed by what we now know about our aunt.

'Who would have thought it?' she says. 'Who would have thought she had something like that in her? Mind you, I always suspected she would turn out to have a secret life. Nobody could really be that boring.'

I suggest that Patricia might not have known what was going on.

'Oh, she knew. She couldn't have been keeping all that stuff in her house without knowing something about where it came from. She'd have had to be short of a few neurons not to know.'

'We always used to think she was.'

'There was a bit more to poor Aunt Patricia than anyone thought.'

I can only agree with her. Even before the latest revelations, I would have agreed.

'Perhaps that's where your criminal tendencies came from.'

We laugh, even though she's not really joking.

My sister brings me magazines, any magazines, usually a small pile of them every time she comes to visit. They represent a world to which I am now a complete outsider; people in restaurants, resorts and their own beautiful kitchens, people with wind in their hair and sun in their eyes, people with smiles on their faces. I leaf through each one from cover to cover – she really could be stealing them from dentists' waiting rooms. I may read a story if it catches my eye, but what I am really looking at is the pictures. When I find one I want, I take my scissors (plastic with rounded edges – impossible to stab someone with) and cut it out roughly along the outline I have decided upon. (I have even been known to send her out for another copy where a picture I want is on the back of one I've already chosen.) Then I spread a large piece of card across my bed and assign each one a temporary position, sticking them with plasticine so that they can be moved around – which they are, frequently. I can spend whole afternoons doing this, moving them from place to place, swapping them around, looking for patterns, resonances, harmonies. I have found myself so absorbed in this process that I have been astonished by the passage of time.

Once I have the layout I want, I perform the final shaping of the image, then glue it into its appointed place. I don't find this process quite so absorbing; it is mechanical in nature and takes place after the creative work has been done. Yes, creative work. It's a term I am not afraid to use. Perhaps, I sometimes think to myself, I too am an artist. I have completed two so far. I stuck them on the wall, next to my cell mate's rather less considered collection of girly stuff, rather to his bemusement at first. Then I discovered him showing them to one of the other members of our unit, and the next I knew they were being exhibited in the common area. They have become quite a talking point.

'I like you Maurice,' my sister now says. She speaks with a measure of surprise, as though it has only just occurred to her that she didn't before. 'You used to be such a stuffed shirt, but you're not now.'

I take absurd gratification from the compliment. I wonder if Patricia would say the same. I wonder if she would still call me pompous. Somehow it seems important to understand that she wouldn't.

My wife came to see me once. She told me that she would not be repeating the visit and she would not be allowing our son to come –contact with him would be confined, for the foreseeable future, to the written word. She brought me papers to sign – I did not even check to see what they were. Divorce, all my worldly goods, a promise not to exist, it was all the same to me. I just wrote my name where she pointed with her freshly manicured nail, using the ballpoint pen she proffered. I signed away my life without demur. It seemed the least I could do.

'I still don't know why you couldn't have pleaded some sort of temporary insanity,' she says as we face each other across one of the little iron tables they have bolted to the floor of the visiting room.

All around us, like the squares on a chessboard, sit frazzled wives and stone hard husbands in similar states of miscommunication, while small children either shy away from their barely known fathers or clamber across them with the single-minded concentration of rock climbers.

'I wasn't insane,' I insist. 'I knew what I was doing.'

'You could have made it much easier on yourself.'

What she means is that I could have made it easier on them. If I had followed the suggestions I was offered, I would have been far more explainable to society. I did make it easier on myself, I want to say. I told the truth. I did not lie.

For the occasion, she had dressed in what I imagine she thought suitable prison visiting gear, a pink outfit she wore for walking, the nearest thing she owned to a tracksuit – I half expected her to turn up with a water bottle as well. She stood out, although not perhaps in the way she might have expected. Most of the other wives had dressed up for the occasion, wanting their men to see them at their best. Tight-fitting dresses, flashing earrings and faces caked with make-up are the order of the day. As she walked away for the last time, watching the lilt of her behind inside the pink pants, I felt the final twinges of a yearning I knew I would never feel again.

She was good enough to accede to one last request. There is a policy here, as long as we behave ourselves, to encourage us to keep pets in the common areas of our units, presumably part of some therapeutic regimen suggested by the prison psychologists. The stipulation is that they must be small and fluffy and able to be kept in cages. She listened while I explained, then nodded gravely and promised to see what she could do. A week later, they turned up, in a brand-new cage painted sky blue – a rabbit and a guinea pig. Thus another ring was added to the prison's concentric circles of confinement, inside the cell, the unit and the prison itself.

The guinea pig is white and russet brown, with long coarse hair that becomes matted if it is not groomed and stands up like a coxcomb if it is. There are no worries on that score; it is always standing up. It has a fat little belly which feels as though it might burst if prodded too hard. The creature is so liberally handled, especially by our youngsters, that I have thought about imposing restrictions just to give it some peace. The rabbit is pure white with no smudges and eyes the colour of stewed plums. It is so tiny, its bones so birdlike, that it is hard to summon sufficient reserves of delicacy to handle it. But we manage. There is a poignancy in the way a man in prison opens a cage.

# 14

It is an evening of damp spring chill when Sandford announces his intention to go up to his brother's house again. This time, he plans a closer look.

'It's Saturday night,' he says. 'They'll probably be out. We can have the place to ourselves.'

'What do you mean, we?'

'You'll drive me up.' It is not a request.

'Are you intending to break in?'

'I want to have a look around, if that's what you mean. I don't intend to break anything.'

Maurice thinks for a moment. 'As long as you don't expect me to go in with you,' he says.

But even as the thought crosses his mind, at the idea of entering someone's house, uninvited, and all the risk this entails, a frisson ruffles his insides, fear and exhilaration in equal parts. Ultimately, though, it is boredom as much as anything else that causes him to give in to Sandford's demand. Saturday has always been a busy night for him. Usually he and his wife are out at a party of some sort or they are entertaining at home – either way affirming their place at the centre of things. Maurice has spent the last three Saturday nights in the house by himself. Even though one day, to someone without work, is much the same as any other, there comes a special restlessness from knowing it is the weekend and that the world outside is making merry without him. He has been thinking of taking himself out for a drive, just to create the illusion of movement, so there seems little reason to pass up the chance of driving to actual purpose.

Sandford collects his bag and they leave the house. Maurice's car is parked directly outside. He remembers the irrational pleasure that morning when he found the empty spot. He has avoided using the car all day to make sure he keeps it.

'Have you got the gun in there?' Maurice hardly dares ask as Sandford drops his bag on the back seat.

'Yes,' he says. 'Want to see it?'

Maurice nods. Not only does he want to see it, he wants to touch it. He wants to feel it in his hand. Sandford reaches behind him and pulls the whole bag onto his lap. He undoes the zipper and fishes around inside. Presently he has the object in the palm of his hand, loosely wrapped in its cloth. Maurice thinks he sees a smile hover around Sandford's lips as he draws back the cloth's four corners. There it lies, settled in his hand, glinting here and there in the light from a nearby street lamp.

Sandford offers it to him. Maurice reaches over. Almost at once, it is nestled in position, its contours perfectly aligned with his own, its weight distributed exactly as his hand would have it, its bulbous sweet spot a foretaste of power against his thumb.

'Is it loaded?'

Sandford nods.

Leaning forward against the steering wheel, Maurice takes aim at the hubcap of the furthest parked car he can see. He dips his head to see along the short barrel. He brushes the trigger. So concentrated are his nerves that it feels as though every tiny ridge on his fingertip is in independent contact with the smooth metal. A squeeze, a tightening of the muscles, a brief signal from his brain to the tendons of his wrist and it would be unleashed.

Now Sandford is removing it from his grip, twisting gently to release it. He places the gun back on its cloth, folds the corners and puts it in the bag, which he then returns to the seat behind him. He does all this without saying a word.

Maurice starts the engine but finds his hand trembling on the gearstick. He breathes deeply to try and calm himself, revving and turning on the radio to hide what is going on. He briefly considers getting out of the car and walking for a while as a way of returning himself to equilibrium, but he knows that if he does this the only direction he could plausibly walk is back to the house, from which it seems very likely he would not emerge. He knows this is what he should do, but the very knowing is what keeps him here. He is being driven by something deeper than simple knowing. He feels infused by a sort of surrender.

On the radio, there is a discussion on the effects of certain mining practices on the water supply of nearby towns. An interviewed woman speaks of her concern for her kids, saying much the same thing to every question. It sounds like she is repeating something she has heard rather than voicing her own thoughts. This absorbs them both for much of the first half of the journey. Sandford does not have to direct Maurice this time. He knows where he is going. The familiar streets and the familiar aggravations of the Saturday night traffic start to soothe him.

They arrive at his brother's street in half the time it took them before. It is immediately apparent that Sandford has chosen the worst possible evening to have the house to himself. His confidence in the unlikelihood of his brother and his wife having a quiet night at home has failed to take into account the possibility of their own house being the centre of things. Cars are parked outside the front, among them an Audi of a similar model to Maurice's.

Sandford is looking around with an alertness Maurice has not seen before. 'Pull in here,' he says. 'In this car, we won't stand out at all.'

'Don't you think it would be better to leave this, do it some other time?' says Maurice.

Sandford takes no notice. 'Pull in,' he says.

Maurice pulls in. Sandford lifts the bag off the seat behind him. They step out onto the road. Sandford closes his door slowly but firmly. Maurice does the same. It is a still night and already they can hear the sound of voices. The two entrances to the property are both blocked by intercom-controlled iron gates and the railings along the rendered wall look too high and too spiky to climb. Sandford, though, has already made his decision. The house next door, which they have parked outside, is quiet, its emptiness attested by the single hall light by which the owners imagine they can fool would be intruders into thinking they are home. Sandford simply opens their gate and walks into their yard. From here, access to his brother's house is just a matter of scaling a wooden fence.

Here they are, standing in the neighbour's yard, gazing up at this large house, this wall from every window of which, once again, light streams forth and through two of which they are able to see the comings and goings of the party. Maurice can discern one end of what must be a big dining room, with a table laid for dinner. There are napkins and candles and glinting silverware. Not so long ago, he would have been laying his own dining table in a similar way. A figure darts in and out in a flurry of nerves, presumably the hostess, the wife of the brother. Hair done for the occasion, long earrings dangling against her cheeks, her anxious, aproned figure reminds Maurice of his own wife's as she prepares for occasions like this. Behind a different window, other figures can be seen. They drift in and out of view, but after standing here for a few minutes, Maurice starts to differentiate them as individuals, from their clothes and the way they walk around.

At one point, three of the men come out from the back of the house, each holding a slim bottle of beer. They saunter so close to the fence that Maurice and Sandford have to duck. One of the men is Sandford's brother. His hair is combed more neatly than it was before and he holds court with a self-assured bearing that brooks no interruption. He is telling the other two about the landscaping in the yard, the reason for their decisions and their future plans. From the tone of the conversation, the politeness of the other two and even the very fact of his showing them his landscaping, it can be surmised that these are not close friends. Quite probably this is their first real social meeting and they are sniffing one another out with a view to future interactions.

Maurice and Sandford watch in silence from behind the fence. The men make a complete circuit of the front yard then disappear down the other side of the house, stopping here and there to inspect some feature or other. Suddenly, light feet scamper up from the gravel behind the house. The dog, excited to have caught them sneaking out, has rushed up and is now starting to leap at Sandford's brother, desperate to be included. Although it passes quite close to where they are standing, it seems oblivious to their scent in its single-minded pursuit of its master. Satisfied now, it trots away into a darker corner of the garden.

After this, there is little movement inside the house. Maurice imagines them serving pre-dinner drinks in one of the other rooms, imagines the hostess appearing every few minutes, flushed and perspiring, pulling her husband aside for a quiet word about some issue in the kitchen. Maybe she will be joined by one or two of the other wives, seizing an opportunity to hide for a while. He cannot see anything from here, but he knows the pattern.

Now they are filing into the dining room. The candles have been lit and the ceiling lights dimmed. Maurice can only see the three figures taking their seats at the table's end, one of whom now has her back to him, but the movement of the others is visible in shadows cast against the wall.

'Right,' says Sandford, 'time to move.'

'Move where?' Part of Maurice hopes he is referring to a move back to the car, a decision to leave the evening as it is, without further incident. Another part is looking for something else, an opportunity to indulge the reckless spirit he has felt growing in him.

Sandford does not answer. Instead he lifts his bag and rests it on the fence crossbeam where, behind the thin foliage of a wisteria spray, they are able to take advantage of some of the light from the upper windows. First he pulls out a balaclava. This is in fact a simple beanie, with crude holes cut for the eyes and mouth. He has one for Maurice too, in the striped colours of a football team. It is not his team, Maurice thinks absurdly, before he pulls it over his head. Instantly he is transformed into a lawbreaker. Now Sandford gives him a pair of gloves, cheap faux leather that hold his fingers like cardboard when he first puts them on but with vigorous tweaking soon loosen up. Lastly, like a perverted Santa Claus, he delves into the bottom of his bag and hands Maurice his firearm. It is a shotgun, runtily deprived of its barrels.

'Where the hell did this come from?' Maurice says, just for the sake of speaking. The shotgun is completely unexpected.

'Ssh!' says Sandford.

It is hard to see in the dim light but the whole mechanism appears quite antique beside Sandford's revolver, antique but strangely satisfying in its simplicity. Maurice takes it in his right hand, balancing it so that the wooden stock lies along his forearm with the butt nestling into the crook of his elbow. He brushes the trigger with his newly gloved finger. The padding gives the impression that it could go off at the slightest touch.

'Don't worry,' says Sandford, as though completely aware of Maurice's thoughts, 'it takes a fair bit of pressure. And yes, it is loaded. You've got two cartridges.'

'What are you expecting me to do with it?'

'Just wave it around. It'll make people do what they're told.'

'What are you going to make them do?'

'Just follow me. You don't have to say anything.'

In all the events that have led Maurice to this moment, it occurs to him now that there has been no specific point when he made a conscious decision to do what he is now doing. The actions he has taken have been the result of not making one, of following Sandford by a sort of default. He is still, he realises, at a point from which he could return. He could give back the shotgun, remove the hat and gloves, return to his car and drive it home. He could spend the rest of the evening watching TV and wake up tomorrow in the same world as he woke to this morning. This would require a decision. He doesn't make one. In its absence, he remains in thrall, as it were, to Sandford, captive to his whims, his plans and anything else he might decide to impose. It gives Maurice a feeling he has never had before. Head on, he is facing the void that opens up when all knowledge, power and control have fallen away, when the only thing he can be sure of is that he cannot be sure of anything. He feels suffused by a strange daring, a sort of courage.

Sandford must have this planned a lot more carefully than he has led Maurice to believe. He now removes something else from his bag. 'A present for the dog,' he says, stuffing a small fleshy bone into one of his back pockets.

Maurice dislikes the thought of the meat staining his trousers. At that moment, a dim flurry of laughter draws their attention back to the house. Through the window, he sees the back view of a woman helping herself to something at the table. While her unseen neighbour holds up a bowl, she wields a large pair of salad servers, raising her arms like wings. Maurice sees laughter rippling down the sheer side of her blouse.

'Come on.' Sandford leads him further down the fence line to a shadowed part of the garden.

There is an old garage here, in the back corner of the block, all cracked fibro and sump oil. This must be one of the few remaining houses in the street from when the suburb was originally built, not yet razed for a huge new palace like the one next door, with its garages and bathrooms and spiv-like bearing. Maurice guesses that it must be occupied by the original owners or perhaps by a young couple who have not yet been able to afford to rebuild. From the fact of it being empty on a Saturday night, he assumes the latter. At a point down here, the fence too is its original wooden version. The beams are rotting, the palings bent and more often than not the nails are rusty and loose. It is a simple thing to sweep some of them aside and clamber through. From the confidence with which Sandford leads the way, Maurice guesses this fence line is thoroughly familiar to him. But he says nothing. Sandford has already forbidden him to speak.

They emerge from behind some low shrubs onto a small, half-lit back lawn. This is a property that lays out its jewels at the front. Back here there is only half as much space and little evidence of the meticulous landscaping through which Sandford's brother has just been conducting his guests. Over in the far corner, a swimming pool lurks behind its fence, water dimly illuminated from below, filter quietly humming. Through the wide kitchen window, they can see the brother's wife hurriedly scrubbing at something in the sink. She has removed her apron. She wears a black, sleeveless dress and her long earrings shake. She is facing them but she does not look up, so concentrated is she on her proprietorial anxiety. Even if she did raise her eyes, it is unlikely she would notice them as they are standing just outside the window's soft crescent of light.

The wife (Maurice hesitates to think of her as Sandford's sister-in-law) now moves away from the sink and busies herself with something out of their view. Sandford steps forwards, into the crescent. He glances around and motions, with a twitch of the head, for Maurice to follow. Maurice takes his own step forward. As he crosses the shadow's rim, he is conscious once again, though less starkly this time, that this might be the real point of no return. He has not yet been seen by anyone and it would still be possible, technically, for him to slink back into the dark, pass through the gap in the fence, return to his car and resume his life. In truth, though, this would mean cutting the invisible thread that ties him to Sandford. This requires a special tool, which at this moment is not available to him. The velvety light, in which he now finds himself, feels as bright against his face as a floodlight in a stadium. He follows Sandford's short, light footsteps to the base of the small covered deck that leads to the sliding doors that lead to the kitchen and then the rest of the house. He notices a brief jutting of Sandford's jaw – the twitch first seen asserting itself in the funeral car when he was deprived of tobacco.

They make their way up the three steps and across the wooden slats of the deck. At the point where he is looking down to establish the position of the back door step, he feels something soft but unyielding in his face. He pulls up, wondering what overhead beam or door frame he has failed to spot in his first quick glance across the scene. It is Sandford's hand, thrust at him palm outwards. He realises this at the same moment his reasoning catches up to establish that no beam or door frame would exist so close to the ground. By keeping his arm extended, Sandford manages to direct him to the wall next to the sliding doors, behind which he is concealed from anyone inside. Sandford now raises his other hand high into the air and, accompanied by what sounds like a low hissing, begins to slowly lower it. Once again, Maurice is confused. For a moment, he thinks Sandford must be indulging in some arcane ritual, perhaps some inversion of a blessing, the import of which will be revealed in due course. Then he sees the dog. Its tail is docked to a stub, so he is not able to tell whether it is being wagged, but it might as well be. Presumably alerted by their scent, it has emerged from the kitchen to the sliding doors where it now stands, in steadily dwindling alertness, following Sandford's rising and falling fingers with its nose as though attached to them by a piece of string.

All the while, Sandford emits the hissing sound, too quiet for anyone else to mistake for anything other than normal background noise, but evidently mesmerising for the dog. In the position Maurice has taken, backed against the wall to the side of the open door, he is now surely in the dog's vision, but it takes no notice of him, directing its full concentration at Sandford's quivering hand as it slowly descends to the level of its snout. When they connect, Sandford deftly moves up his fingers until he is caressing the dog's silky brown forehead. At the same time, with his other hand, he is exposing the bone. This he now brings up under the dog's chin as though offering it a ministrant tissue in which to spit some indigestible shard. The dog, with one, then two tentative bites, takes the meat in its jaws, looks up for a second, then trots down into the yard to enjoy it, just outside the crescent into which they have so recently stolen.

'I'm family,' Sandford explains quietly. 'It recognises my smell.' He wipes his gloved hand on the back of his trousers and regrips the revolver, temporarily stowed in his other back pocket. He nods at Maurice. It is time.

*

Maurice crosses this last threshold with barely a thought. Much of his attention is absorbed by the feel of the shotgun and its weight on his arm. It does not feel like something that could be held anywhere other than its point of equilibrium. The existence of the breaking mechanism seems to demand that it be balanced, and he has it in place along his forearm, leaving the other hand free to keep him steady as he climbed through the fence, across the uneven surface of the yard and up the three wooden steps. The last time he remembers holding something this way, it was his infant son. He is treating the shotgun with a comparable reverence, mindful of the potential damage if he were to stumble. Now, however, he is in the light, on an even and reliable surface. He can hold it with both hands, a pose that seems more familiar from films and TV.

They are in the big bright kitchen. It is part of a larger room, divided by a wide granite bench top lined with stools whose legs are bound with solid but decorative ironwork. (Maurice's wife once bought something similar for their kitchen but changed them after a year or two.) In the white-tiled living area is a familiar combination of couches, home theatre equipment and children's toys. The party is taking place in the more formal section of the house, where they are in time to see their hostess disappearing, through a doorless archway on the other side of which emerges the unmistakable aura of social gathering; flickering candles reflecting brittle chit-chat across an underlay of soft music and spicy smells.

Sandford starts immediately through the doorway behind her. He walks, Maurice would even say he strides, with such nerve and sense of purpose there is nothing Maurice can do but follow in his wake. If he had thought about it, he might have been struck by the sheer contrast between the Sandford of this moment and the Sandford he had first known. He might have looked for connecting threads, clues that might have prepared him for what he now sees. But at this moment his mind is a blank. It is ready to be impressed with a whole new set of truths.

Sandford catches up with his brother's wife just as she is entering the dining room. She must have heard something. She is about to turn when he places his left hand over her mouth and pushes the revolver into the side of her neck with his right. He does all this with more force than seems necessary, but this very brutality reduces her to an immediate state of submission and creates a sufficient window of hesitation among the others – alerted to the attack by the sound of the bowl in her hands smashing on the parquet floor – to show them that there is now no in-itiative to be gained. They shuffle into the room ahead of Maurice, a strange four-legged beast with a fragile facade. Her earrings flicker like horses' tails as Sandford forces her into the position he wants. Maurice has never felt so helpless as he does now, watching this happen.

Eight places are laid, all but one of them taken. The first thing that catches Maurice's eye is that the four men have their elbows up on the table, with fingers variously clasped together, while the women sit with their hands in their laps. Is this, he wonders briefly, something he should have noticed before, something fundamental to the gender divide? Their main look is incomprehension, perhaps even a refusal, or at least a re-luctance, to believe what they are seeing. This does not last very long. In a few moments, they have assumed the individual tonicities that will carry them through the events of the next ten minutes. A blonde woman in a yellow dress gives a short, nervous shriek, as though she is about to pass out. One of the men opens his mouth but does not speak, while another starts to shout pompously – yes, pompously – demanding to know what they think they are doing here. This is the first time Maurice has seen Sandford's brother up close. He sees little resemblance between them. Lead-grey strands in his hair vaguely echo Sandford's, but he is balding from the front where Sandford doesn't appear to be balding at all and his dark brown eyes contrast sharply with Sandford's, which have very little colour. Furthermore, the whole shape of his face is different, more pink and smooth and full, although how much of this could be attributed to his relative prosperity is difficult to judge at this moment, for Sandford's masked features do not lend themselves to more detailed comparison. The blonde woman, seated next to him at that end of the table, collects herself now and glances around. They all watch, mouths open, closed, trembling, hardly daring to move. Sandford, again more roughly than is necessary, now pushes the wife down into the empty chair, where she sits, shaking slightly, her face partly screened by misplaced locks of hair.

'Shut up!' he shouts, holding out the revolver for all to see.

His brother continues talking, so he aims it towards him. Now he does stop, but with reluctance, it seems. Maurice is impressed by this, an action born of common sense rather than fear.

At this point, Sandford glances over and asks Maurice, in neutral tones, to turn on the lights. Maurice reaches behind him and finds the switch. Until this moment, all the lighting, apart from the candles, has come from a pair of standard lamps in opposing corners of the room, but now it all seems drowned in stark white light. Suddenly, all the lines on all the faces become visible, the colours stand out in the women's dresses and bald heads shine on two of the men. Maurice wonders whether the presence of this light will be matched by a clarification of Sandford's intentions, but he just stands there surveying the scene. The blonde woman, he now notices, is not really blonde. Her eyebrows are dark, though clipped, and shady undertones show in her hair. She stares at Maurice, and her pearl necklace trembles slightly against her skin.

Her husband, shorter and goateed, places a hand on her lap. 'What do you want?' he says. 'What do you want from us?' He speaks without inflection, but his voice is clear and strong.

Sandford does not answer. Instead, he strides slowly the length of the room and it occurs to Maurice for the first time that he has no plan. He does not know what he is going to do.

The brother, meanwhile, has collected himself for another speech. 'You know you're not going to get away with this,' he says, 'so here's my offer. Walk away right now and we won't pursue it. Walk away and it'll be as though none of this ever happened.' His voice has the high, toneless ring of one who is not certain how his words are going to come out. His cheeks colour as he speaks, mortified no doubt at his inability to control it.

Sandford looks at him. 'Who are you to be making offers?' he says quietly.

There is something of the same ring in his voice, which confirms two things to Maurice, that they are related and that he is nervous too.

'You're invading my house.' His brother speaks more steadily now. Perhaps he has heard the quaver in Sandford's voice and is encouraged. 'It's a very good offer.'

'It's your offer,' says Sandford. 'What about the others?'

There are one or two tentative nods among them. The woman seated next to the brother's wife, up at Maurice's end of the table, is shaking her head to herself, in some private paroxysm.

'You!' Sandford shouts.

Everyone jumps, as though shocked by the same electric bolt. The woman, whose top appears to be made from iridescent scales, looks up.

'What about you?'

She looks at him but does not speak. The scales on her top change colour as she moves. Evidently she had not been listening.

'None of us will say anything,' says Sandford's brother. 'I give you my word.'

For the last time, Maurice sees the glimmer of a threshold. Remote as it seems, here once again is a chance to walk away, to go back and carry on with his life. Granted, it would require the cooperation of every person in the room but it is still a chance, and he experiences once again the strangely compelling taste of abandon as Sandford's response closes the door for good.

'Your word?' he almost laughs. 'What is the worth of that?'

He walks the length of the room and back. He holds the revolver awkwardly, as though unsure of the correct grip. It seems more alarming this way than if he was comfortable with it, giving the impression that he might do anything, that he is not in total control. The three with their backs to him, none of whom has spoken so far, are unable to follow his movements without shifting in their seats. None cares to do this for fear of drawing his attention. They look down into their laps, at Maurice's end one of the men without hair, next to him his wife, overweight and anxious, and at the other end, next to Sandford's brother, another large man whose collar is already damp with sweat. The married couple exchange a quiet look, a mixture of fear and reassurance that does not go unnoticed by Maurice.

While this is going on, the blonde woman, the one on the brother's left, has been looking more and more feisty. Maurice has noticed the hardening of her jaw, the way her eyes have narrowed into openings through which tiny darts could be fired. He has learned to steer clear when a similar look appears on his own wife's face.

She starts to speak. 'I wouldn't let you walk out of here,' she says firmly.

The trembling of her pearls against her skin, Maurice now recognises, had been a trembling of intent, not terror.

'How dare you walk into people's houses waving that…thing about?' She flicks a dismissive hand in the direction of the gun, as though unable to find words to sufficiently describe her contempt for it.

Sandford turns to look at her. It is hard to tell whether he is taken aback. Maurice certainly is. He hopes she will keep her scorn focused on Sandford. At the same time, an obscure part of him feels aggrieved that she has not even appeared to notice him. Before Sandford can respond, his brother's wife speaks from the other end of the table.

'I agree,' she says. 'Who the fuck do you think you are?'

The scatology sounds foreign to her lips, as though it is language she is deliberately using to place her at one step removed from this situation – it reminds Maurice of his own wife's use of the term fuck buddy. If she had been seated in her place she would be facing away from him, but she is still where Sandford thrust her, facing half out from the table, and she is able to include Maurice in her disdain. At the other end of the table, the brother closes his eyes as if in pain.

'Why do you have to hide your faces?'

'Haven't got the guts to show them,' the stout woman murmurs, almost to herself.

In the ensuing silence, her words hang in the air. The blonde woman gives a quiet, appreciative nod. Would they be more respected, Maurice wonders, without the masks? For a mad second, he wonders whether removing them would turn back time.

'Shut up,' says Sandford. His command is effective because it is delivered in a measured voice, accompanied by fresh gesturing with the revolver. First he points it at the stout woman, who is facing away from him and doesn't see, then, briefly, at the blonde woman, and then at his brother, who reacts by raising his hands, palms out, in front of him.

It is a gesture more of supplication than surrender, an instinctive desire to calm a beast that has been inadvertently aroused. Maurice sees the flickering of the tic traverse the skin of Sandford's throat.

'What have we done to you?' the man says. This time, in addition to his brother's eyes, he looks into Maurice's.

Maurice stares back, feeling the full protection of his mask. His words have been spoken in panic, given away by the almost complete disappearance of the last syllable before it leaves his mouth.

Now he blusters, attempting to reassemble his position. 'Look, I don't know who you are, but why don't you just take whatever it is you want and leave us alone?'

'What do you want?' the goateed man asks.

Sandford lowers the gun. He appears to be thinking. 'What I want,' he says, 'is for you to do what you were doing before I came.'

Everyone looks puzzled now, as would Maurice if his face could be seen.

'Do you mean, just before?' someone says.

'Yes,' Sandford says impatiently. 'Just now, before I arrived. What were you doing?'

Wives and husbands now exchange glances, looking for guidance. They still don't understand. There is a roll of the eye, a quiet sucking of teeth, but they are careful to do this outside Sandford's field of vision. His unpredictability, now it has become clear, seeps through the room like a dangerous new gas.

'What were you doing?' Sandford says again. He is now looking at his brother.

'We were just…chatting,' his brother says.

'All right, keep on chatting.'

'What do you mean?'

Maurice notices the puckering of the brother's cheeks as he briefly allows for the possibility that this might all be some sort of joke.

'Exactly what I'm saying. What were you talking about?'

'I don't know, the markets, I think. Or was it the golf?'

'It was both,' says the large man sitting next to him. 'We were wondering which way interest rates were going to go. Before that, we were talking about golf, about the Masters.'

'Well, keep talking,' says Sandford. 'Carry on with your conversation about interest rates.'

The two of them look at each other. The large man says he expects the next movement to be up, the brother agrees, then the words dry up as Sandford turns on the blonde woman.

'What about you?' he says.

'We were talking about schools,' she says, indicating her side of the table, her goateed husband and the woman in the iridescent blouse.

'Schools. What about them?'

'The good ones in the area. They have a little girl,' she indicates the couple across the table. 'She's starting school next year, we were talking about it.'

'Well, keep talking.'

'This is ridiculous!'

'Do it!' He points the gun.

'Actually,' says her husband, 'I think we'd finished that conversation. We were just making general remarks about the food.'

'Keep doing it!'

They glance across the table, where various dishes quietly steam. There are crinkled poppadoms stacked in little baskets at either end of the table. On the floor near Maurice lies the rice which was scattered when the wife dropped the bowl.

'I have to go and check on my child,' she says suddenly, rising from her seat.

'Sit down!'

She remains poised. 'I've got to. I've got to see if he's all right, I've got to go.' She raves to herself, shaking her head and covering her eyes.

'He'll be all right,' Maurice says. It is the first time he has spoken.

She looks up at him. 'You don't understand,' she pleads, 'I have to go.' She stands.

'Push her down,' Sandford says firmly.

Without a thought, Maurice finds himself pushing the woman back into her seat. The shotgun brushes her stomach. Speaking has made him want to prove he is alive, that he is feeling and responding. He would like to take the woman out to see her son. But at the touch of the shotgun she resumes her seat with the obedience of a dog responding to years of training. At the other end of the table, her husband makes to move. Then he looks at Sandford, whose muscles have visibly tensed around his revolver, and he stays where he is.

Suddenly, Sandford raises his voice. 'Talk!' he commands. 'Why have you stopped? I want to hear you talking. You, talk about schools. You, talk about money!'

'I think we'd finished that conversation too,' says the large man, holding out his empty hands.

'Well, talk about something else then!' Sandford is shouting now, almost screaming.

He pushes his gun into the back of the man's neck. Then, instead of tensing up under the feel of it, the man seems to relax completely. He glances across at his wife, the woman in the iridescent blouse.

'I'll tell you what,' he says, in a voice turned rich and mellifluous. 'I'll tell you about our holiday…'

All eyes turn to him as he starts to describe, in the sort of detail nobody would ever normally presume at any social gathering, the dash to the airport, the tedium of the check-in and the security screening, the waiting amidst the duty-free stores, the call to board, the queue, the wrestle to their seats, the stowing of the hand luggage. By the time he reaches the safety demonstration, his wife has started interrupting him, just as though this is a normal holiday anecdote, to remind him of little details, to colour in between the lines he has drawn with perceptions of her own. On and on he talks.

Maurice can see what he is trying to do. On behalf of everyone else, he is taking on the burden of responding to their presence, and especially to Sandford's bizarre and capricious impulses. It becomes oddly mesmerising listening to someone relate something so unexceptional in such exacting terms. After a while, Maurice finds himself fascinated by the detail the man is presenting and it occurs to him that it is just as valid to relate something common and ordinary, such as this, as it is to relate the extraordinary and the sensational. Either way, the audience receives that person's perceptions, and these are extraordinary in themselves because they are unique to them. And this man is not unskilled in the art of anecdote.

Sandford seems to be feeling something similar. He stands quite still, letting the man continue through the plane flight, the meal, the landing, the passage through customs, the selection of a taxi and the journey to the hotel. For seconds at a time, Maurice forgets that he is an intruder in someone's home with a deadly weapon in his hands. Meanwhile, the food steams, uneaten, on the table, the wine remains unpoured and the poppadoms lie stacked in their baskets like the brittle layers of memory and perception.

It is the blonde woman who awakens them out of what can only be described as their stupor. At a suitable pause in the proceedings, after they have given their conflicting views on whether it was necessary to tip the man who carried their bags, she decides to open her mouth.

'I hate to interrupt,' she says, 'but are we going to sit here listening to this all night or are you going to do whatever it is you came to do and leave us in peace?' She seems to have quite recovered her poise.

Maurice realises that for some of them it could be unbearable, the limbo into which the man's anecdote has placed them. Clearly, though, she is making an assumption, concerning Sandford's intent to use his weapon, that could be considered rash. Or perhaps she has thought carefully and has come to the conclusion that this is a reasonable tactic to employ at this point. Or perhaps, and if she had been Maurice's wife this would undoubtedly be the case, she is unable to prevent herself giving rein to her natural impatience. She glares at Sandford fearlessly. A brooch in the design of a beetle glints near the neckline of her yellow dress.

'You're right,' says Sandford. He takes a step forwards and traces the oblong perimeter of the table with his gun hand. 'I want all your valuables – watches, jewellery, wallets, everything on the table in front of you.'

Nobody moves.

'Do it!' Sandford shouts.

The man who has been telling the story is the first to respond. Shifting in his seat, he removes a slim leather wallet from his back trouser pocket and drops it on his empty plate. There it lies with its corners upturned like a large, thick leaf. He then wrestles the watch from his left hand and places it on the wallet.

'What about the ring?' says Sandford.

'I don't know if it'll come off,' he says.

'Take it off!' Sandford unlocks the catch on the revolver. Its weighty click takes more than its share of the room's reverberations.

The man begins struggling with his ring. Meanwhile, like tentative drops at the start of a rainstorm, there come the sounds of hard objects being cast onto china here, there and eventually all around the table. Rings, pearls, earrings, bracelets – soon every plate is filled with these things in a sort of uneatable parody of what should have been there. By half closing his eyes, Maurice can imagine it as food, with the wallets as slices of meat. Some of the jewellery, it is immediately obvious, is of no value. But even if every one of the wallets was stuffed with notes, the total value would go nowhere near justifying the risk Sandford is taking by bursting in here with guns. He is only asking for these things as a nod to expectation. His real agenda is somewhere else.

He strides up and down inspecting the haul. The large man is still struggling with his ring. He tries to do this discreetly, down on his lap, but Sandford insists he keeps his hands on the table. The man's wife is still wearing her earrings, black pendulous objects in the shape of stick figures.

'Take those off,' he says, now pointing the gun at her.

'But they're not worth anything,' she says.

'Doesn't matter. Do it!'

She unhooks the earrings and places them on her plate next to her bracelets. Then she starts shaking out her hair, the beginnings of what must be an instinctive reaction to the disencumbrance of her face, before she remembers where she is and reddens.

Meanwhile, Sandford is turning his attention to the blonde woman. 'What happened to that thing you were wearing?' he says, gesturing at his own chest.

'What thing?'

'For Christ's sake!' says the brother. 'Haven't you done enough? Can't you just take what you've got and go?'

Sandford ignores him. 'It was a little creature, an insect or something,' he says. 'You had it pinned up here.' He points carelessly with the gun. 'I want it on your plate!'

She gives a single turn of her head – the slow, tentative beginnings of a shake. She is wondering whether to bluff it out. Her goateed husband tries to catch her eye but she doesn't look at him.

'Show me your hands.'

She presents them as fists, and uncurls them to reveal nothing. Her bare arms look creamy in the harsh light. Sandford's throat gulps again.

'I don't know what you're talking about,' she says, more slowly and deliberately than would be the case if she was telling the truth. Not only has she decided upon this course, in her defiance she is prepared to do so in the full knowledge that he knows she is lying. She is bluffing it out, but she is challenging him too.

He looks at her for a moment. The balaclava masks the expression on his face, so this showdown is only marked out by a moment of stillness across the room. 'Take it off,' he says.

'What?' She curls up her lip in an expression borrowed from a teenager. Insolence is the effect but there is no hiding the shudder that concludes it.

'The dress.'

'Oh, come on…' the brother says, but is silenced by the gun, this time suddenly trained on his head.

'Go on, take it off!' He is still trying to sound like someone prepared to wait all night if necessary, but his creeping impatience is betrayed by the quick, edgy movements of his hands.

The woman now pulls something out from under her dress's neckline. It is the brooch. She presents it briefly in an open hand before dropping it onto her plate with the other things.

'Take off the dress,' Sandford repeats, slowly and clearly.

'There's nothing else,' she insists.

'Do it!' He raises the gun and pulls back the catch. But he does not aim it at her, he aims it at his brother.

Sweat beads across his brother's forehead. The blonde woman, in a pose with which Maurice has become familiar through many years' watching his wife, reaches behind her back with both hands and loosens the zip that holds her dress together. This is the point at which his wife would normally ask for his help, but she manages it on her own, drawing it down in two stages, one hand parting it to the level of her shoulder blades, the other taking it down to her waist. She looks at no one. It is almost as if she is in the privacy of her bedroom. Maurice is not aware of any other movement in the room. The dress is now fully open. She unhooks it from her shoulders with each hand in turn. It drops, but not without a light, unseen tug to get it down below the level of her flesh-coloured bra. There she stops, thinking this might be enough.

'All the way! Drop it on the floor behind you.'

Trying not to leave her seat, she pushes the material down over her hips, flexes her stomach and lifts herself a few inches off the chair for the remainder of its journey down to her feet. Then she leans over, picks it up and drops it behind her, as she has been told. She sits there in just her bra and underpants. The underpants are white and brief. On all the flesh she has just exposed is evidence of the complexion she has managed to conceal with creams and make-up – raw-looking blotches and a handful of dark moles, their prevalence only accentuated by the rose-coloured flush that now veils her from head to toe. She sits there with her eyes closed. If she is hoping now to avert further attention, she is to be disappointed.

'What are you stopping for?' he says. Now he aims the gun straight at her.

She opens her eyes and gives a start. There is an audible sigh from somewhere else in the room while she sets about complying with his demand, once more reaching both hands behind her back. This time her action is accompanied by a single toss of the head, a gesture that sweeps her loose hair back across her shoulder. It is intended to display her unbroken pride but it doesn't, quite.

As she does this, there is movement, a minor commotion, from across the table. It is the large man, the one who told the story about the airport, wrestling himself out of his own shirt. It is a finely striped business shirt and he is wearing it with the sleeves rolled up, exposing his hairy forearms. He pulls the tail out of his trousers and begins to undo the buttons, starting with the ones around his stomach. His fingers are large and ungainly, and where the buttons give him trouble he simply yanks it apart.

Sandford turns. 'What are you doing?' he says. For the first time, his voice is that of someone not in control. As if in elucidation, the tic ripples across his throat.

The man takes no notice and continues to wrestle his shirt away. He frees one arm, revealing a plump, white, hairy breast. Across his forehead now hang several damp locks of hair which had formerly covered his baldness.

'Stop!' Sandford cries. 'Stop it!' He waves the gun.

The blonde woman's goateed husband now removes his hand from his wife's lap and begins to unbutton his own shirt.

'No!' Sandford cries again. He is now pointing the gun at anything that moves. 'You,' he aims at the blonde woman, who is poised with her bra unclipped but not yet removed. 'You, keep going!'

She remains as she is. The men continue to undress. Sandford's brother looks as though he might be about to join them. The woman in the iridescent jacket has acquired a steely look, as though she is weighing up whether to pitch in too. Sandford darts this way and that, quite unsure for a moment which way to turn. Finally, he stands still, straightens his right arm and fires a bullet into the centre of the table.

So sudden and fierce is the sound that in the ensuing silence it is hard to believe it has happened at all. It seems to have altered the very structure of the room's atmosphere. Silence now builds itself like a wall around the violent, fleeting crack. Its only physical trace is a broken dish in the middle of the table and a smell more sharp and pungent than any curry – that and the pinned, frozen faces of the diners. The dish, though shattered, has retained its shape. Brown sauce seeps from its base and forms slowly billowing shapes on the surrounding cloth. For the next few minutes, Maurice hears the ringing in his ears.

'Now,' Sandford says, in a voice straining for calm, 'everyone does what I say.' He breathes heavily, twice.

No one moves. Then, in almost the same moment, Maurice catches something, a presence, in the corner of his right eye. The mask restricts the range of his vision, so he turns his head and sees, framed in the archway, the figure of a child. The child is standing just outside the light but can be seen to be wearing blue fleecy pyjamas with a pattern of clowns and balloons, and to be holding by the ears a soft toy, a stuffed animal so well handled it is almost devoid of its insides. The toy is held against the child's cheek with the same hand that provides the thumb for its mouth, while the fingers of the other hand twist ringlets in a dishevelled dark mane. He – it is a boy – stares up at Maurice, in the way of a small child, with eyes wide enough to accept all possibilities. Maurice remembers the smell of sweat that used to radiate so sweetly from his own sleeping son. Any day now, he thinks, the boy's father will be insisting on a haircut.

What is Maurice to do? He is a grown man, standing here in this child's home with a mask over his face, holding a loaded twin-barrelled shotgun, with his ears still ringing and his nostrils tingling from a bullet that has just been fired in his name. But he wants to lean over and inhale this child's scent. Suddenly, he sees himself through the child's eyes. Quite probably the gun and the covered face would be so far outside his experience that they would only be interpretable as a game; dress-ups or some other form of make believe. It is the covered face that most seems to assault the child's pureness. In his world, there can be no just cause for an adult to cover his face like this. Without another thought, Maurice is pulling away the balaclava and dropping it on the ground. He is gratified to see slight movement across the boy's cheeks, the beginnings of a smile. Maurice is now something he can comprehend, something he can take into his world. He moves into the waiting arms of his mother. At the same moment, Maurice becomes aware of the other sounds in the room, as though a station has just been picked up on a radio dial.

Sandford is shouting. He is ranting and raving at Maurice. His voice has shed all its diffidence and restraint. It is the voice of an animal. At the same time, his brother has risen to his feet.

'I know you!' he cries, making repeated jabs across the table with his pointing finger. 'I know who you are!'

Is he referring to Maurice or Sandford? In the confusion, it is hard to know.

More quietly, to his right, another voice has been calling the child's name. It is not a command, the voice has the tone of someone who is not sure where to find the person they are calling. A figure fumbles through the archway and stands, blinking, where the child stood a few moments ago. It is a woman, an aged relative presumably, brought in to babysit while the parents entertain. Her grey hair streams across her shoulders ready for bed. With her other hand, she holds something together across her chest, a shawl or a cardigan. She stares in Maurice's direction. Her tiny black eyes are like holes in her thin face. Her mouth opens, then closes without utterance.

'You!' The brother rises to his feet and starts to walk towards where Maurice is standing.

Maurice feels an urge to repeat the word back to him to see if his own voice sounds the same.

Sandford fires again, this time into the ceiling. Plaster sprinkles the table and a cloud of dust billows down in easeful contrast to the force of the bullet. Such is the commotion, and the collective gasps and screams, that it's hard to register these all as separate sounds. The blonde woman is taking the opportunity to re-cover her breasts. The child climbs onto his mother, all the while staring mutely back across his shoulder. The old woman penetrates Maurice with her eyes. From different directions now, Sandford and his brother are bearing down on him. They march in strange unison, in a shared gait that marks them as family. The child screams for the first time. He has dropped his toy.

And if Maurice is asked whether he regrets the events of the next few seconds – those actions for which he refused all pleas from temporary insanity to self-defence – whether he regrets his finger's almost instinctive caress of the hard locked trigger as the brothers rage towards him, the momentary gasp of fear as he tests its resolve and the absence in him of a decision not to squeeze and squeeze and squeeze, he cannot truly say that he does.